JORDAN AND THE DREADFUL GOLEM

Karen Goldman

Illustrated by Rachel Moseley

Penlight

To Arnold:
Thank you for your love and devotion
and for strengthening my light.

Jordan and the Dreadful Golem
by Karen Goldman
Illustrated by Rachel Moseley
Paperback edition – 2014

Text Copyright © 2014, 2013 by Karen Goldman
Illustrations Copyright © 2014, 2013 by Rachel Moseley

Typeset by Ariel Walden

Printed in the USA

ISBN 978-098-386-854-5 (softcover)
ISBN 978-098-386-852-1 (hardcover)

Penlight Publications
527 Empire Blvd. Brooklyn, NY 11225 Tel: 718-288-8300
www.PenlightPublications.com

Contents

Chapter 1

In the Beginning

H I, I'm Jordan – Jordan Gavrieli. I live in Israel. You've heard of it, right? It's a thin strip of land between the Mediterranean Sea, Egypt, Jordan, Syria, and Lebanon. I live in a village called Kfar Keshet. Keshet means rainbow in Hebrew, the language we speak here. Miss Sara, the founder of our village, named it that because a rainbow is a sign of hope. Miss Sara's hope is that through careful training, we, the children of the village, will develop skills to defeat our enemies. It's a long story. I'll tell you about it sometime.

Kfar Keshet is a great place to live. It's in the north of the country, above the city of Tiberias. We have a dam and a lake. And we have the Jordan River flowing right down from the Golan Heights, that plateau at the southern end of the Lebanese mountains. We can see the mountains to the north of the village.

You haven't heard of the Jordan River? There's a song about it that everyone knows. "The Jordan River is deep and wide . . . dah, dah, dah." Anyway, in Hebrew, we call the river *Nahar Yarden*. When Miss Sara named me, she named me after the river. I don't think too many kids in the U.S. are named after rivers. I've never heard of a boy named Mississippi.

Miss Sara names a lot of the kids in our village. She has a special genius, because the name she gives the kids always relates to their gift. Around the age of thirteen, sometimes younger, the kids she has named discover they can do amazing things.

I'm almost thirteen. Just a few more months. I don't have my gift yet. I'm trying to figure out what it will be. I want to be able to fly, like Superman. Up, up, and away.

That's why I'm standing in this tree. I'm working on my gift. I don't have the flying down yet, but I'm getting closer. You see, I'm only wearing swim trunks and a tee shirt. No shoes. I don't want any extra weight.

I scramble up higher. I spread my arms like wings and take off, pushing away the branches. I'm sailing. Then I'm falling. I need lift. But instead, I crash out of the large sycamore with a thunderous rush of leaves and shattered branches and hit the grass, belly first. Oomph. Then my forehead hits the ground.

"Ouch!" I yelp. I hold my head in my hands. Colored dots are racing the Grand Prix in front of my eyes. I shake my head. Another bump on my forehead.

"Jordan! That's the fourth tree you've fallen out of today. You're always falling out of trees."

That's Ziv, my brother. He's two years younger than me. He doesn't know anything.

"I'm just practicing," I tell him for the one hundredth time. "When I find my gift, I know I'm going to be a super-hero. I'm gonna be able to fly."

Ziv shakes his blond head like one of those Bobblehead toys that has a spring for a neck. "You're named Jordan. Come on! What does flying have to do with the Jordan River or water?"

As I push the hair out of my eyes, I accidentally touch

the new bump on my forehead. I take a deep breath and hold still so Ziv won't see I'm in pain.

"There must be a connection," I say. "You just don't see it. What do you know, anyway?"

"I know my gift," Ziv says, in his snotty way.

I look down, and my shoulders slump. It's true. Ziv knows his gift even though he's younger than me. Sometimes it seems like everybody else gets things first.

"Sorry. I'm sure your gift is going to be great," Ziv says.

"Yeah, I've waited long enough. Let's go for a swim. I'll race you," I say. My head is spinning like a whirling pizza crust but it won't stop me. I'm Ziv's older brother. I have to beat him at something.

נדב

NADAV

Chapter 2

Trouble at the Lake

"YOU can hardly stand," Ziv says, frowning.

"Yeah, so?" My tanned legs shake as I stand, but I'm two years older and a head taller than Ziv. I take off and leave him in the dust. It's no contest. As I race toward the lake, Ziv struggles to keep up.

We speed past the rushing, tumbling Jordan River, the river I've been named for. I sprint uphill past the hydroelectric dam to the deep lake above, my legs no longer shaky. I can hear Ziv huffing and puffing behind me.

Under the eucalyptus trees near the water's edge, I yank off my shirt. I head straight for the water and dive in. Sweet! The cool water tingles on my skin. I flip onto my back like a seal and float lazily on the surface, my eyes closed. The summer sun warms my belly.

Ziv finally arrives. I hear him stripping off his clothes and open my eyes. His pink stomach jiggles like Jell-O as he walks to the water's edge. He slowly lowers his toes into the lake like it's shark infested. He doesn't love water like I do. I stare at the wide blue sky. After a while I hear loud splashing and furious kicking.

"Just let the water carry you," I yell without looking up. "You sound like a drowning cat."

"Shut up, brain-starved!" Ziv yells back.

I shoot up from the bottom and spray him with a huge mouthful of water. I'm laughing. I fill my mouth again. I see my friend Noam coming by. His name means pleasant and agreeable, just like soft clouds in a bright blue sky. He's the kid who knows how to form clouds. He can do some really neat things with them – like making shade by covering the sun with a cloud. I swim close to the shore and shoot a mouthful of water at him. He's always so cool. The spray splatters his skinny legs, but he doesn't laugh. His usually smiley face looks like the underside of a black cloud.

"What's up, Noam?" I shout.

"Nothing," he answers through gritted teeth.

Ziv and I glance at each other, and then scramble out of the lake.

"What's going on?" I bounce on my right leg to shake the water out of my ear.

Noam growls his answer. "I've been collecting tadpoles all day for my summer science experiment. I have a special jar for them with a really tight lid. One of the kids over there took it, and I don't know who."

I look across the lake, and see trouble with a capital N on the other side. The N stands for Nadav. He's the principal's son. A lizard begins leaping around in my stomach. There's going to be a fight. I hate fights, but my friend is in trouble. I look over at Noam's angry face. I huff out a breath. I can't let him down. Can't chicken out.

"I have an idea who did it," I say. A knight's squire appears in my head and clothes me in armor. I'm ready for a fight. "Come on. We'll get them back." Noam's face lightens like a clear sky after the clouds have disappeared.

We cross the red footbridge to the other side of the lake. I expect to hear my armor squeak and clunk, but all I hear are our feet slapping against the wooden planks. We head to a small stand of eucalyptus trees. The tall boy with black, eerie eyes stares at us. They are so black his pupils have disappeared.

I grit my teeth and step up to him. "All right, Nadav, where are Noam's tadpoles?"

Nadav inches closer to me. "Why ask me?"

"'Cuz you're always picking on somebody."

"Go whine to your mother," Nadav sneers.

My armor melts away. I'm defenseless. I feel naked. Finally I think of something aggravating to say. "Maybe I'll speak to your father, the principal." I straighten up as tall as I can.

Nadav's dark, black eyes glare at me. Then his voice becomes all sugary and he asks, "Did ya figure out your gift yet? Hard, isn't it?"

It's as if a knife cuts out my throat. I can't speak. His black eyes seem bottomless.

Nadav laughs under his breath. "Some kids just don't have gifts, you know. Maybe you're one of those regular kinda guys. It's okay. You don't have to be embarrassed."

There are some kids without gifts. Nitzan, who's almost fourteen, hasn't gotten a gift yet. He might not be getting one. I heard Miss Sara didn't name him. I swallow hard. Hot-faced, I glance at Noam and Ziv. They've heard Nadav. Neither one looks at me. They're busy studying something on the ground.

I curl my fists and step closer to Nadav. *I don't want to fight, I don't want to fight*, a voice says in my gut, but there's no way out of this.

Nadav juts out his chin and stares at me.

We move toward each other, as though in a dance. Our chests are almost touching. I look straight into his eyes.

He lifts his balled fists. I crouch, ready to spring.

Noam and Ziv jump forward. They grab me by the shoulders.

"Forget the tadpoles," Noam shouts.

I try to fight them off. They pin me to the ground. Pointy pebbles dig into my shoulders.

Nadav steps back. "Not cool," he says. He cackles a short laugh and raises his hands in surrender, mocking me. Then he ducks behind a tree and reappears with Noam's jar of tadpoles. "Take the dumb things."

Noam grabs the jar from Nadav and jumps back.

"It was only a joke," Nadav calls over his shoulder as he walks off.

No one laughs. They pull me up. My body is still shaking but I can stand upright now, and I push my shoulders back. I glare at Nadav's back as he retreats toward the village.

We walk back across the bridge without a word.

At the swimming spot by the eucalyptus grove, Noam slaps me on the back.

"Jordan, you're the greatest," he says. "You stood up to that creep! Awesome!"

I stare at the dried-up eucalyptus leaves on the ground. I'm pleased we got the tadpoles back, but I feel like a relay runner who's dropped the baton. Maybe Nadav's right and I don't have a gift coming.

"I'm gonna take the tadpoles home," Noam says. "See you tomorrow." He waves, tucks the jar under his arm, and heads for the village.

I plunk myself down on the riverbank and shove my hot feet into the water. Sweat drips down my forehead.

"I have a feeling you're going to get your gift really soon," Ziv says.

"You and your feelings," I mumble.

"Don't knock it. It's my gift."

I'm silent. I have nothing to say to him.

Ziv waits a second for an answer then finally says, "I'm going home. See you."

I grunt good-bye and hear my brother walk off.

I pick up a fallen branch from one of the eucalyptus trees

and beat out my frustration. I stretch forward and write the word 'gift' in the mud with the tip of the branch. I stare at it.

"Hey, Jordan."

I look up. Ellah is coming. I jump up and kick the dirt to erase what I wrote. Then I wave to her.

"How ya doing?" she asks as she slides down next to me.

"I'm okay." The words feel like sand in my throat.

"How 'bout a swim?" She smiles.

"Maybe later."

"What? You love to swim. Dare you." She jumps up and runs toward the lake.

I sigh and stand. I kick the branch away and follow her.

גברת שרה

MISS ✦ SARA

Chapter 3

Meeting Miss Sara

THE next morning I stare out my bedroom window at the trees in the front yard. I'm tired of falling out of them. I want my gift.

Noam has his.

My little brother, Ziv, has his and he's not even thirteen.

Ellah has a thing with spiders. That could be hers.

Maybe falling out of trees has made me brain dead. I have to check. I once heard my parents tell someone it's the first thing to go.

I sit down at my desk and leaf through the booklet I brought home from my visit to the Air Force Museum at the Hatzerim Israeli Air Force Base. It shows all of the aircraft in the Israeli Air Force. I cover the names of the airplanes with my hand and quiz myself.

I do pretty well. I correctly identify the Boeing F-15, the McDonnell Douglas A-4 SkyHawk, and the Beechcraft T-6, and all the other planes. I'm feeling better. I flip to the page showing the helicopters. These are really hard and I make one mistake. I think the Boeing AH-64 is the Bell 206. But I ace all the others. My brain's still working. I put the booklet in its place of honor on my desk, between my alarm clock and my picture of Abba and Ima. That's Hebrew for Dad and Mom.

I hurry to the lake. It's another hot day at the edge of summer. Ziv is already there. I leap into the cool water with a tremendous splash. Deep, deep down I go, like a nuclear submarine. A small minnow darts past and I grab for it. Its slippery body slides through my fingers. I smile and wriggle toward the surface. Air bubbles tickle my skin. As I take a deep breath so I can dive again to search for more minnows, someone calls my name.

I spin around in the water. On the high bank, Miss Sara, the village elder, waves at me. She smiles her welcoming smile and motions for me to come out of the water. She is wearing a green and honey-colored dress that covers her knees. Sunlight shimmers through her white curly hair and sparkles on the star-shaped sapphire necklace around her neck.

I smile and wave back. My heart is beating wildly in my chest.

Maybe today I'll get my gift, and fly.

With long, smooth strokes I pull myself through the water. At the shore I scramble up the bank. With shaky hands I dry myself as fast as I can and slip on my shirt and sandals. I approach Miss Sara, a knot in my chest. My legs feel wobbly like when I fell out of the tree.

Let this be my day, I'm saying to myself over and over. Let this be my day.

Miss Sara steps forward to meet me under the eucalyptus grove. I smell the familiar sour odor of her wool clothes. Politely, I shake her cool, dry hand as I've been taught. Everyone honors Miss Sara. She founded our village a long time ago.

"Good afternoon, Miss Sara."

"Jordan, your time has come."

My knees go rubbery. I hear my heart pounding in my ears.

"Come with me." The village elder watches me intently, like a wise owl.

I turn for a second and search for Ziv. He's down the shore, splashing water at his friends. I call his name and signal that I'm going with Miss Sara.

Ziv flaps his arms up and down like a bird and winks at me.

I grit my teeth. My face burns and my earlobes turn hot. They're probably red as strawberries. Ziv's going to tell me afterwards that he had a feeling that today was my day. No time to think about that now. I wave and turn quickly to follow Miss Sara as she leads me from the lake and downhill past the dam toward the Jordan River.

Let this be my day.

Miss Sara's sandaled feet kick up swirls of dust along the path. We pass the massive concrete dam that generates electricity for our village and three others nearby. After a few minutes of walking in silence, Miss Sara stops at a bend in the river where three trees have created a shady corner. She brushes aside some early fall leaves, and with a deep breath, eases herself down on the riverbank, sitting cross-legged a few feet from the rushing, tumbling, white-capped Jordan.

I sink down beside her. Shaking with excitement, I kick off my sandals, scoot down closer to the river's edge, and push my toes into the chilly water. The Jordan rushes past, burbling and bubbling, swirling leaves in its wake, noisy and full of life. My heart pounds. While I sit and wait for whatever is going to happen, I scratch out small pebbles from the bank and toss them into the water.

Miss Sara clears her throat.

I dart a glance toward her. "I hope you're not going to tell me school's starting a week early." I crunch my face into a pretend frown.

"Not to worry," Miss Sara says. "The teachers are anxious to start, but we're holding them back so you'll have one more week of freedom."

"Hurrah!"

Miss Sara smiles.

I smile back at her, but I feel my lips quivering. I stop picking out pebbles.

"Jordan, in a few months you'll be thirteen. Soon you'll be considered a man in the eyes of the village." I scoot closer to hear her every word.

"It's really time for you to discover your special ability."

Discover? Disappointment trickles through my chest. I frown.

"What's wrong?" Miss Sara asks.

"I've been hoping I'd be able to fly."

Miss Sara shakes her head. "I don't think so, dear," she replies in her soft voice.

Words start plummeting out of my mouth, one after the other. "You know I'm ready to help people, right?" I lean forward, eager for Miss Sara to hear me. "Remember, I caught little Eden when she got too close to the Jordan? Just think if I could fly! I'd fly over from school in a second and save people. Wouldn't that be great for the village?"

Miss Sara waves a pesky fly away. "I'm pretty sure that water is your medium, Jordan."

"I know I'm named Jordan, but maybe it isn't something to do with water. Maybe . . . maybe it means—" I stop to think for a minute. "Maybe it comes from the word *yarad* . . . like to fall down. Maybe falling down is like flying."

I look hopefully at Miss Sara. She raises her eyebrows and shakes her head.

I spread my arms wide. "I was meant to fly."

"You'll fly when you get into the air force."

"I hope so, but that's not till I'm eighteen. I want to do it now."

Miss Sara shakes her head again.

"Maybe you made a mistake when you named me."

Miss Sara's mouth falls open. "No, Jordan, I did not," she says in her strictest voice.

I feel my neck getting hot. I'm sure it's as red as a beet. My words come out scratchy. "I just thought that maybe I got someone else's name, you know, someone who was born at the same time as me."

Miss Sara stares deeply into my eyes and says nothing.

"There wasn't anyone else born then?" I gulp.

Miss Sara shakes her head.

"Maybe I don't have a special gift. Have you ever named a kid who didn't have a special gift?"

"No. Everyone I name has a special gift." Miss Sara smiles gently. "Those born with this gift have the ability to clear their minds and become one with and influence nature. That is why your names are so important – they connect to the particular aspect of nature you connect with."

I sit up straighter. "I didn't know that."

"Yes, it's an ancient wisdom. All of the children are taught techniques that the elders of our people have gleaned from studies of Kabbalah and other mystical sources."

I feel my chest swell. "Kabbalah," I whisper. "It's such an amazing study and I've been part of it." My mind flashes back to nursery school. I remember we all had special *hugim*, lessons. We did a lot of wordplay, adding and subtracting letters to make new words out of old ones. It was fun.

"Was it all of those word games we played in nursery school?" I ask.

Miss Sara's gray eyes sparkle. "You've been in training for a long time."

"So the gift we get allows us to become a natural part of the whole universe?" I smile, remembering. I was really good at those games.

"That's right. You're one of the lucky ones who will have

this talent. I was guided to name you Jordan, which must mean your gift has something to do with the Jordan River, or with water."

I start to disagree, but Miss Sara puts up her hand. "Let's get to work," she says.

I look at my toes in the water, then at Miss Sara. "I do feel happy when I'm in the river," I say in a resigned voice.

"Good." Miss Sara pats her white curls and gives me a look as if she's seeing beyond my body and into my brain. "Now all we have to do is figure out exactly what your gift is. Noam discovered his gift by speaking a lot about the sky and clouds. During our talk he learned he could create and manipulate cloud formations."

"So you want me to talk about the river?"

She leans closer, one eyebrow raised. "Yes. I do."

"Well, I really like the color blue. You know, the sky is the same color as the river. That's why I thought I'd be able to fly. When I'm swimming, I imagine that I'm floating through the sky. I'm sure that I'd move my hands and feet in the air the same as I do in the water. Swimming is a way to teach me how to use my hands and feet in the sky, to fly."

Miss Sara looks disapproving, but she doesn't say a word.

"I love to look at the clouds reflected in the water."

Today there are high wispy clouds in the blue sky. I hear Miss Sara's gold bracelets jingle as she picks specks of dirt off her dress. I pull my toes out of the water and spin myself around to face her again. "I remember in school, when we learned about the second day of creation, the words were something like . . . 'There was water above and water below the earth.' Doesn't that sound as though the sky could be thought of as a river?" I smile at her.

Miss Sara looks at me. "Interesting. I know which verse you mean. I never thought of it that way."

I straighten my shoulders. Now we're getting somewhere.

Miss Sara frowns. "But you need to forget that, Jordan." My shoulders sag and my head drops.

"Concentrate more on the river and less on the sky. Tell me about you and the river."

I let out a breath. I don't want to disappoint her. "Well, it's great to dive into the water on a hot day. You get cool really fast."

"Anything else?"

"When I dive in on a hot day, the water covers me, like, like another skin . . . like it attaches itself to my body. Does that sound stupid?"

Miss Sara sits upright. "No, not at all. Now we're on to something. Go on."

"Well, I like to chase the little minnows because I feel like I'm just like them, a fish. Except I have arms and legs. So I should be able to catch them with my fingers, but they usually get away."

"Great!" Miss Sara claps her hands.

My heart is pounding. Maybe I am getting closer. The words spill out. "In the water I feel weightless, like my body is somewhere else and all I have are my eyes and ears attached to my head, which is somehow part of the water. Like being weightless in space."

Cloud shadows begin to form on the water. It's close to lunchtime. I hear my friends leaving the lake and heading home. I sit waiting, listening to the whisper of the water brushing along the bank. I feel a slight gripping in my stomach, like the current is pulling at me.

Then I hear Miss Sara's deep sigh. "I think you need to express your connectedness with the water more, Jordan," Miss Sara says. I can hear the disappointment in her voice.

I shoot to my feet. "This is so hard! I want to fly. You want me to be a fish." I pull off my shirt and dive into the water. I sink down and the cool, clear water envelops my body. I swirl my hands back and forth like waves, rising up and down. I swim in large circles like fish do. After what seems like an hour I drag myself out of the Jordan. The water hasn't revealed any of its secrets.

I plop down next to Miss Sara again. She seems to be studying the sky. It's like I don't exist. Drops of water trickle down my face.

Miss Sara says nothing.

I stare at the ground. "I can't think of anything else. I tried to focus on the water . . ." I shrug. I'm sure water isn't my element.

Miss Sara gently touches my shoulder. "Your water gift hasn't come yet, Jordan. I know it will. I think you need some time by yourself to think about your gift and what we said here today."

For the first time ever, I find it hard to look Miss Sara straight in the eye. I've let her down. I'm a failure. Her lips are pressed together and she keeps her eyes fixed on the sky. I feel invisible.

"Jordan," she says.

I look up.

"It's time for me to go home." She stands up gracefully and brushes the leaves off the back of her dress.

I scramble up, feeling like a fish out of water that's gulping for air. I shake Miss Sara's hand and watch as she climbs the riverbank and heads toward the village.

I kick at the ground, blinking frantically a number of times. I don't want to cry. The water dripping down my legs makes me shiver. I want to leave this river and never return.

Just then Ziv walks up, kicking pebbles with his sandaled feet. "So, Jordan, what's your big secret?" he asks, bobbing up and down like a Bobblehead toy.

"Shut up," I snap.

Ziv stops jiggling and stares at me. "Sorry," he says. "I just thought . . . I just thought– I mean, I saw you with

Miss Sara and I thought . . . you know . . . I thought you found your gift."

I grab a stone and set it skimming across the water. "Well, I didn't," I say. "Let's go home."

We climb the bank.

"Hey!"

We both look up. It's trouble. Nadav is sitting with his legs twisted around the branch of one of the trees. I don't need this.

"How'd it go, Jar?" he sneers. "Did you get your gift?"

My hands tighten into fists. Does the whole world know? How dare he call me Jar instead of Jordan! "I'll kill him," I growl.

Nadav chuckles. "Hey, Mr. Tadpole-saver, rescue me! I think I'm going to fall out of this tree."

There's a whoosh overhead. I look up, past Nadav, as though he's gone. An F-15 races high above. Its chem trail puffs out the back. I don't feel any excitement at seeing the plane. Today is an epic fail.

Chapter 4

The Last Camp-Out of the Summer

"*D*ON'T forget to put on your mosquito spray. Don't burn down the forest. And don't unroll your sleeping bags on top of anthills."

Ima rattles off a list of instructions to us. She's always nervous before we go into the woods. Ima is what we call our moms in Hebrew.

"Don't go to sleep with dirty hands," she adds, with her hands on her hips.

"Don't worry, Ima," I say. "It's our third sleepover in the woods this year. We'll be just fine. I'll see to that."

Ziv nods beside me.

"Did you take flashlights? What about binoculars?" The equipment list continues.

I roll my eyes. "We've got everything. It's only one night. We'll be back tomorrow."

Ima stands on the front steps and waves good-bye as we hoist our backpacks and sleeping bags on to our shoulders and leave for Noam and Ellah's house.

"Sometimes Ima makes me crazy," Ziv mumbles as we leave her behind.

"She just worries about us," I say. "We're going to have a great time. Did you remember the marshmallows?"

"Duh, of course."

"And the matches?"

Ziv flashes me a look. "Are you scared?"

"What do you mean?"

"I dunno. You know sometimes I get a feeling about something. While we were eating breakfast I had a feeling like something was holding on to my throat and—" Ziv grabs his throat.

"Oh, it's just because you don't like granola. If Ima had made pancakes you would have been just fine."

"I don't know. It felt pretty real to me." Ziv studies the ground.

I never know what to do when Ziv gets one of his feelings. "Come on. Noam and Ellah are waiting."

We race each other down the three blocks to Noam and Ellah's house.

When we arrive, Noam is in his backyard, as usual. He's wiping the lens on his telescope. He spends a lot of time looking through it. Thank goodness he's not bringing it with him this time. A month ago it almost fell into the lake in the forest.

"Ready?" I ask.

"Yeah." Noam covers his telescope with plastic sheeting.

"Where's Ellah?" Ziv asks.

"She's under the trees looking for some spiders."

"Of course," Ziv says.

"Ellah, come on! Jordan and Ziv are here!" Noam yells into the air.

Ellah skips out from around the side of the house with a mason jar in her hands. "Look! Aren't they amazing?" She swings the jar, crawling with spiders, right in front of my face. She knows I hate those disgusting things. I step back and look away like I'm interested in the sky.

Noam chuckles. "She got you again with that spider jar in the face," he whispers.

I shrug like it's nothing and say, "Come on. We're ready to go."

"Hold on." Ellah runs into the house. In a few minutes she returns with her backpack.

Noam and Ellah shoulder their camping equipment and wave goodbye to their mother.

"Don't forget—" she starts to say, but the rest of her words are drowned out as we all yell good-bye.

We follow the deer trail across the grassy meadow. It's the end of summer. The grass has faded from lush green to a dried-out yellow. Once we're past the last meadow of Kfar Keshet, the pine trees thicken and close in around us. Into the woods we go. We're silent for a while. We hear the rustling of lizards in the grass. The only other sounds are the snapping of dried twigs as we step on them and the swish of bushes as we shove them aside.

The trees are top-heavy with green needles. The ground is dry and dusty. We march along, stopping occasionally to drink from our canteens. I like the forest. It's quiet. I can breathe deeply and smell the musky air. I feel my heart-beat slow down.

"I thought the forest would be cooler," Noam says, brushing sweat off his forehead.

"We'll be at the lake in no time," I say. "You'll get to take a dunk."

"I don't know about that," Ellah says. "That lake always looks pretty algae congested to me."

"Girls!" We three guys say in unison as we march on.

"Boys!" Ellah snorts in response.

A low green bush with red berries stands out among the green leaves. "Hey, look at those berries." Ziv points. We stop for a minute and pick some of the berries.

"They're poisonous. Don't eat them." Ellah puts a hand on my arm. "I'm pretty sure they're yew berries and they're really dangerous."

Ellah knows a lot about plants. While Noam gazes at his clouds, Ellah pays attention to the earth. So we listen to her.

We drop the berries like they're radiating 220 volts of electricity and squash them with our shoes. *It's good that Ellah knows so much about plants*, I think. But I don't say it out loud.

After a couple of hours of walking through the quiet woods, we reach our destination.

"There it is!" Ziv whoops.

Overgrown willows and green spiky sedge grass surround the lake. Frogs croak. A hidden creek gurgles nearby as it empties into the lake. We clamber through the tall waving grass in a hurry to get to our favorite campsite.

We rush around the south side of the lake and stop suddenly, gasping in surprise. A large black ground cover is spread over our place, a black duffel bag on top of it.

"Darn it," Noam curses. "Someone's taken the best spot. What should we do?"

Ziv grabs at his throat. "Maybe we should go home." His voice sounds like a frog.

"Don't be dumb," I say. "We'll find a place on the other side of the lake. No one owns it, you know."

We walk half a kilometer around to the far side of the lake. The view is different from here. It doesn't feel the same. My chest is kind of heavy. I wonder if Ziv's nervousness is rubbing off on me. About six meters from the lake, we find a good place to camp. It's not as close to the lake as we'd like, but there's a clearing where we can safely light our campfire. We can't see who stole our campsite, and they can't see us. I drop my backpack and sleeping bag. The others do the same. I peel off my shirt. Before I dive into the lake, I watch as Ellah tromps off into the woods. She isn't afraid of anything. I'll bet she's after some more disgusting spiders.

The lake is waiting. I take a running start and jump feet-first into the cool, deep water. Splashing and yelling, Ziv and Noam follow me.

After our swim, we pitch our tent and lay out our sleeping bags. Then we eat dinner around the campfire – the best kebabs, roasted potatoes and chocolate s'mores. Mom's food is the greatest. My stomach is full. I pat it gently.

As the sun sinks, darkening the forest around the lake and around us, the nighttime gurgles of small frogs and the buzz of mosquitoes get louder. We're about to begin singing some camping songs when suddenly there is a loud hissing and banging coming from the other side of the lake.

We all jump. Now what? I'm thinking. This place is usually so quiet you can hear the stars spinning.

"Anyone want to see what's going on over there?" I ask.

"No," Ellah says at once. "It's scary."

"Don't chicken out." I stand. "You know we always take a night hike on our camping trips."

Ziv and Noam are all for it and Ellah finally agrees.

"Get your binoculars and flashlights. Let's go," I say.

With my friends marching behind me, I lead the way along the curve of the lake to the abandoned stone house on a little hill overlooking the dark, still water.

"From here we'll see who stole our campsite," I whisper as we approach the unlit stone house.

We step through the opening where there used to be a door. This place has been abandoned for so long. It smells like rotten leaves and moldy earth. We all huddle together in front of the two big glassless windows and stare out at the lake.

Near the water, a man wearing a white robe is sitting cross-legged next to a fire. The flames sparkle and dance off the silver headdress on his forehead. The headdress has a large star right in the middle.

"Cut the flashlights." My voice shakes as I give the order.

Everyone clicks them off. My eyes adjust to the dark. We're shadows against the black walls of the cabin.

"Who is that?" Ziv whispers. We crowd at one of the windows. Noam and Ellah watch from the other window.

"Some weirdo," Noam answers in a low voice.

"Let's get out of here," Ellah whispers. "That strange man is making me nervous."

"Don't worry, I'll protect you," I say as bravely as I can.

"No! I want to go!" Ellah says loudly. Her voice quivers.

"Shush," Ziv cuts in. "If he hears us, we're dead."

"We'll go soon," I say.

"Okay, soon!" Ellah whispers.

Silence fills the place, as if we're in a horror movie.

The strange man fascinates me. I stand still as a statue and watch him. "Hand me the binoculars. I want a closer look." I hold out my hand to Ziv.

"Where are yours?" Ziv asks.

"I forgot them at the campsite. I can hear Ima complaining already," I say with a little nervous laugh.

I tug at the strap around Ziv's neck.

"All right. Hold it! You're choking me." Ziv lifts the binoculars over his head.

"Thanks," I whisper, and raise the binoculars to my eyes. "He's grabbing some dirt," I announce. "He's raising and lowering the dirt like he's praying or something."

"Now he's washing his hands," Noam says, staring through his binoculars. "Look, he's got a tattoo on his right hand."

"Really?" I say, shifting the binoculars. Then I

see it. "It's a tattoo of a full moon with a star above."

"Is he the bogeyman?" I ask in a whisper.

"You mean Lavan, the one they say does all kinds of weird magic tricks?" Ellah's voice is shaky.

"I remember someone said Lavan has a tattoo on his hand," Noam says.

"That guy has one." The tattoo on his claw-like hand sends shivers up and down my spine. We all stand in silence.

"Lavan is a magician or something, right? No one has ever seen him but everyone's afraid of him," Ziv says.

"Do you think he'll be mad at us if he finds us staring at him?" Ellah asks.

"What can he do to us? It's a free world. " Noam's statement hangs in the air.

"Maybe he eats people?" Ziv coughs, choking on his words. "I told you I had a bad feeling about this trip when we were having breakfast," Ziv says.

I nod. The hike was my idea. If anyone gets hurt, it's my fault. My heart pounds like a bongo drum in my chest.

Then Noam asks, "What's he doing with that huge book?"

"Let me see!" Ziv grabs for the binoculars and I give them back. Ziv whispers, "He's really being careful with it. It's wrapped in plastic. He's unwrapping it and putting it on the ground cover."

"To keep it clean," Ellah whispers.

"Ya think?" Ziv jokes, but we don't laugh. He hands me back the binoculars.

Noam sneezes and the sound echoes through the stone hut.

The man stops reading the book and jerks his head toward the house where we are hiding. I pull my head back from the window, like a turtle. We're all holding our breath.

"Whoo!" An owl hoots in a tree nearby. The man turns

his head and listens for a moment and then returns to his book.

I let out my breath carefully. Everyone else starts to breathe again as well.

I peer through the binoculars. "Hey!" I whisper. "Showers of sparks are leaping up from the book! How does he do that? He is running his finger down the pages and as he does that, sparks jump up everywhere."

Ellah, Ziv, and Noam all crowd together at the window for a better view.

"Scary! Let's go," Ellah says.

"Now he's just sitting there," Ziv says. "Is that it?"

I shake my head. "He's kneading that whole pile of dirt like Ima kneads the challah dough. He's adding water with that empty Cola bottle. What's he making?"

"I'm cold," Ellah says. "Let's go back to the campfire where we can warm up."

"Wait a second. We've watched this long. We've got to stay to the end," I say. My brain is buzzing. I keep asking myself, what is he doing? We can't leave. Not yet.

The sound of a Hebrew song fills the night air. I've never heard the melody or the words before, but it reminds me of the prayers on Shabbat in our synagogue. The man sings it over and over. "*Golem, golem shel olam, amod yashar, v' azor li.*" (Golem, golem of the world, stand up straight and help me.)

I'm shivering. My ears are ringing, and my eyes are locked on the strange man. I understand what he's saying, but what does it mean? What's a golem? Cold fear sweeps over my body.

Chapter 5

Mud Man

WE stand with our eyes riveted on the scene, hardly breathing, like we're glued to a fast action movie. No one speaks. Ellah stops asking to go back to the camp. It seems like it's been hours since we first saw the man, but it's probably only been ten minutes. We can't turn away.

The man washes his hands, sits back down at the fire and reopens the book. The dirt and water he was kneading are now formed into shapes, pieces. He arranges them on the ground next to him and sprinkles water over them.

He sings again, and his voice gets louder and louder. The words are all a jumble. I don't understand them.

Noam sucks in a breath. "The full moon is shining on the exact spot where the dirt pieces are. That star near it is Venus."

"The full moon and the star. Just like his tattoo," I say. Shivers attack me again, up and down my spine.

"Aaaiiieee!" Suddenly the man lets out a shrill scream. My heart stops beating. Ellah, Ziv, and Noam crowd closer to me, grimaces of fright on their faces.

An owl hoots and then stops suddenly. A frightened field mouse skitters into the run-down house and runs over Ellah's boot.

"Eekkk!" she yells.

"Oh my God. He's coming," Ziv whispers fiercely, looking through the binoculars. "We have to get out of here."

We all run out the door and into the woods. Then, like a bunch of monkeys, we scamper up the trees.

I watch, sitting one third of the way up the tree, by the light of the full moon. I don't need binoculars to see the man.

He creeps toward the house. At the threshold, he stops and studies the matted grass at the doorsill. He kicks the earth with his boot heel, peers into the darkness and then slips inside. Crunch! He must have stepped on Noam's flashlight; I dropped it when we rushed out. I hear him slam his boot down. There's more crunching, like he's grinding the pieces into the earthen floor.

He steps outside, red-faced and scowling, and paces around the cabin, examining the ground. He mutters and growls.

Up in the tree, behind the cabin, I grip the branches. My heart is beating as fast as a hummingbird's. What will he do to us if he finds us? How can we save ourselves? Through the leaves I see him still standing beside the building. He's swaying back and forth as if in a trance. He looks from the cabin to his mud piles a few meters away. A moment later he kicks the earth again and hurries back to the lake edge and the mud.

We're all quivering with fear. I wait for what feels like half an hour and then I signal for everyone to come down. We slide out of the trees. Silently I lead everyone back into the cabin so we can watch the man again. No one protests.

I'm praying that no one sneezes or yells again. I'm praying the man doesn't return to the cabin. We gather next to the windows like before.

"What's he doing now?" Ziv whispers.

I raise Ziv's binoculars to my eyes and tell everyone that the man is circling the dirt piles.

Rays of moonlight sparkle off his white robe. He lifts the star headdress from his head and clutches it in front of him. Then he starts plodding in circles around the dirt shapes, his mouth moving. We can't hear the words. He must be whispering.

We count aloud in a low voice. One, two—seven times around. That's how many times a bride walks around her groom under the wedding canopy. Then the man drops to his knees suddenly, and shakes his hands to the sky like he's calling to the heavens.

There is a sudden crack of noise, sharp and loud. Light flashes like a strobe light. We all jump and gasp. A bolt of lightning pierces the air and zaps the large piles of mud. An electric charge crackles in the air. The man leaps to his feet, waving the star headdress. Now he's dancing in circles around the piles, which glow like neon lights.

My throat is as dry as desert sand. I look at my friends. Their hair is standing on end. I guess mine is, too. Small sparks of electricity snap between our fingers when we move our hands. We're stunned. There's no rain. No thunder.

A fog begins to swirl around the man. Through the fog, I can barely make out the dirt mounds, but it seems like they are creeping towards each other. Arms, legs, a head, and a body are forming. The man is singing a low, prayerful song. His voice breaks. He takes a deep breath and resumes the song. He drops to his knees again and starts yelling unrecognizable words.

Then I see something through the binoculars that makes me gasp.

"What?" Ziv whispers.

"He's made a man. He's crawling on his knees toward it," I say in a shaky voice. "He's—he's speaking to it."

"I can't watch!" Ellah stumbles back from the window opening. Beside me, Noam and Ziv are goggle-eyed, too.

"Ugh. He just gouged out eyes, a nose, and a mouth." I feel a bubble of nausea rising in my throat.

Ellah is drawn back to the window as we watch the man lift each hand and foot and inspect the fingers and toes. He touches the body and straightens the hair. Then he backs away from the figure and claps his hands. The figure turns its new head toward the sound.

"It looks like a grown-up baby," Ellah says, holding Noam's binoculars.

The figure slowly sits up. The man gestures to it, and it stands up, on what seem to be shaky legs. The man removes some clothes from his duffel bag and quickly dresses his new creation in pants and a button-down shirt.

"He knew what he was doing," I whisper. "He even brought clothes."

The man snaps his fingers. His creation bends to pick up the book the man was reciting from, the duffel bag, and the ground cover. Then the man points and the creature walks, heavily, away from the lake. The man follows close behind.

Dazed and shaken, we're unable to speak. Our backs against the stone wall opposite the windows, we slip to the dirt floor and sit, holding our knees. I slowly thaw out. After a while I notice the sounds of the forest animals. I stick my head out the door and check to the right and left.

"It's time to leave," I whisper to the others.

My friends rub their arms and legs as though they've fallen asleep. They slowly rise and stumble out of the cabin.

"Come on. We've got to get back to our camp," I urge.

My friends are impossible. They straggle behind me, stumbling over tree roots and small patches of briars. Their teeth are chattering. I hear them turning every few seconds to make sure we're not being followed. I do the same.

"I told you we shouldn't have come. I knew there was going to be something scary," Ziv says in my ear.

Shivering even though it's a warm night, I whisper, "I know, Ziv. I know."

A million questions zoom through my head. What was that thing? How did the man create it? What can it do? Maybe we're in danger. I need my gift now.

Chapter 6

At the Campfire

WHEN we reach the glowing ashes of our campfire, we search for more logs. Everyone wants a huge fire. When it's roaring again, we sit down close to each other, shoulder to shoulder.

"What was that?" Noam asks, his voice shaking.

The four of us stare into the fire.

"Let's go home," Ellah suggests for the hundredth time, her voice high and tight.

"We can't. It's too dark to see the way," I say.

An owl hoots. We start, look around wide-eyed, and then resume staring at the fire again.

"It's scary here," Ellah whispers.

"We have the campfire. We'll be safe." I try to reassure her, but I'm scared, too.

"Did we really see that?" Ziv asks.

"Well, we sure didn't imagine it." I reach over and throw another log on the fire. A flame shoots up, big and sparkling, reaching for the stars. "Kebabs and potatoes can't make you hallucinate."

Noam giggles nervously.

"We saw a man make a man. A real live, breathing, moving man from mud," Ziv says.

"No one's going to believe us," Noam says.

"There's one person who will," Ellah says. "Miss Sara. We must tell her what we've seen. I'm sure she'll know what happened here. She'll believe our story."

She's right, of course, and we all agree with her.

"In the morning, okay?" I say, looking at my brother and my friends in the glow of the campfire.

Everyone nods.

An animal scurries through the underbrush. Ziv jumps. Our friendly forest is now a scary place.

Warmed by the fire, we all begin to yawn, but nobody wants to go to sleep.

I make the first move and stand up. "Time to turn in, guys."

The four of us rush to the tent and slither into our sleeping bags.

"I'll never fall asleep. Everything is just so crazy," Ellah says.

"How 'bout a ghost story?" Ziv suggests.

"No way!" Noam howls.

"Don't yell. He'll find us," Ellah whispers.

"He's far away from here. I'm sure we're safe now." I stifle a big yawn.

"I hope so," Ellah says.

Noam's eyelids blink and blink again. "It's kind of hard to stay awake."

"Yeah." My voice sounds heavy in my ears.

After a while, I hear Ziv's heavy snuffling and Noam's soft murmurings. At least they're asleep.

The forest night sounds make my skin crawl. I can't help but imagine that crazy man sneaking up on us. I squirm out of my sleeping bag and crawl outside. I inch forward, hugging the side of the tent. An owl hoots. Electric shivers race up my spine. I look up at the dark night sky and the trees around us. As I slowly turn my head, I spot something in the tree to the left of our dying campfire. I duck down and stare at the shape. It's too big for an owl. What is it?

I look at the tent door. There's no way to slip back inside without being seen. As I hold my breath, pressing against the base of the tent, the figure slides down the trunk of the tree and disappears into the forest.

It's Nadav.

I swallow down the sour taste of shock and disgust and slip back inside the tent. Slowly I worm back into my sleeping bag. I punch the bundled-up parka under my head and stare at the dark tent ceiling. I'm trying to figure out why Nadav was sitting up in that tree. As I lie there I hear Ellah clear her throat.

"Are you awake?" I whisper.

"I . . . I'm so scared," Ellah blubbers.

"Wait a minute."

I grab my sleeping bag and parka and drag them over to Ellah. I lay my bag next to hers and bunch up my parka again so we can both pillow our heads on it. I zip myself into my sleeping bag and reach over and take her hand. In a few moments we're both asleep.

Chapter 7

Miss Sara Hears the News

"YOU children are sure back early from your camping trip," my mother says to us as we drag ourselves into the house early the next morning.

I can't tell her that we were all too scared to spend any more time in the woods. As soon as the sun was up we packed up our campsite and hurried back to the village.

"Didn't you have a good time?"

"It was okay. We just got sort of tired of the lake. It's really algae infested," I say.

She looks at me suspiciously. "You always liked the lake, green or not. Did something happen?" Ima sets down the newspaper she was reading.

"Nothing, Ima. Nothing happened. We just decided to come home early." Ziv smiles sweetly.

"Okay. Put all the camping equipment in the shed. Don't leave any lying around."

We give her an army salute, three fingers over the right eyebrow, and drag our backpacks and sleeping bags to the shed in the backyard. Up in our rooms we strip out of our dirty clothes and take turns jumping in the shower.

As I pull on clean clothes, I'm thinking about the tattoo on the strange man's hand. Moon is *Levana* in Hebrew.

Levana, Lavan. Could it be? We all know him as the big baddie. Ima and Abba used to scare us into doing things by whispering his name. I fall into my desk chair in disbelief. Sand fills my brain and for a while I think of nothing at all.

An hour later, as we all agreed, we meet at the far end of the village, near Miss Sara's cottage. She's feeding her sheep in the grassy sheep pen in front of her house. When she sees us she pushes away a black ewe nuzzling her, opens the wooden gate, and steps out to the garden path.

"It's a lovely day," she greets us. "How was your camping trip?"

Miss Sara always knows when we go into the woods.

"We had the weirdest experience," Ellah says.

Miss Sara looks closely at our pale faces. "Sit down," she says, pointing to the grass. Shaded by the nearby bushes, we sit in a semi-circle facing her. "What happened?" she asks.

"This is going to sound hard to believe." I begin telling her about our camping trip, and the mysterious man who took our usual spot next to the lake.

Miss Sara stops me as I am describing what the man was wearing.

"*Who* did you see?" She asks like she didn't hear me.

"A man in a white dress . . ." I repeat.

Miss Sara looks from face to face.

We all nod.

"What did he look like?" she asks.

"He was tall and thin, with sandy-colored hair," Ziv tells her.

Miss Sara sits up straighter, her face pale. "Anything else?"

"He had a tattoo on his hand," Noam says.

"You could see it?"

He nods. "It looked like a full moon with a star above it."

Miss Sara bites her lip, but says nothing, so I continue

telling her what happened. What the guy had with him, and how, while we watched, he gathered clumps of dirt, kneaded the dirt like dough, chanted and added water, and sang and danced.

"We watched while he created a man," I finish, and sit back, my throat tightening as I think of the weird man.

Miss Sara is rocking back and forth. I've never seen her like this.

"Miss Sara, are you all right?" Ellah asks.

"No, I'm worried." Miss Sara straightens her spine. "Could he have been doing something else? Maybe you didn't see clearly."

We all shake our heads. "He created a man. A real living, breathing, walking man. He played with the dough and he made something alive." I shiver and throw up my hands. "Gives me the creeps!"

"Honest. Give us your Bible. We'll swear to it," Ziv says.

Miss Sara shakes her head like she doesn't want to hear what we're saying. Sweat glistens on her forehead. Her face is as white as boiled rice.

"He did it like this, Miss Sara." Ziv stands up and starts rhyming nonsense words while he dips and sways and dances around the lawn.

"Enough!" Miss Sara whispers fiercely.

Ziv quickly sits down.

Miss Sara slumps her shoulders. For a moment she's still and silent. Then she looks us each in the eye. "This is very serious. This golem is a danger to all of us."

"Golem. Yep, that's the word he sang in his song," Ziv says. "What's a golem?"

He asks the question I want to know, too.

"Oh," Miss Sara moans softly. "Why did I say that?" She opens the door to her house and asks us to follow her inside. She heads straight for her office. From a high shelf she pulls down a large green book and blows a thick layer of dust off the cover.

"He had a large green book, too," Noam points out.

Miss Sara nods. "I know." She lays the book down on her walnut desk and opens it carefully.

We pull extra chairs around her desk and watch as she slowly turns the large, yellowed pages. The book is filled with strange writing and diagrams. I've never seen anything like this before.

"What is that book?" Ellah asks.

"It's a book of ancient wisdom." Miss Sara turns another page. "I fear my brother Lavan has been using it."

We all cringe. We've always been taught that Lavan is the bogeyman. Whenever something bad happens we blame Lavan. We're shocked that Lavan is her brother. This is really scary.

Miss Sara opens the book near the end and flattens down the pages. I can read the chapter heading: "A Golem."

"Here is the information." She runs her finger down the page and begins to read aloud to us.

"The most famous golem was created in the late sixteenth century by the chief rabbi of Prague. His name was Judah Loew Ben Bezalel. He was also known as the Maharal. He created a golem to defend the Prague ghetto from anti-Semitic attacks."

We sit wide-eyed, listening. It's the first time we've heard about the golem and the Maharal.

Miss Sara continues. "The golem was made out of mud. It was created to help people in distress."

I sit up straight. "Like me and the other kids." I try to smile. "We were all made to help people in distress."

"That's why you need to discover your gift," Miss Sara says quietly.

My throat tightens and I look down at my shoes.

"How can someone create a man out of dirt?" Ziv asks.

Miss Sara points at the open pages. "Lavan studied this book for a long time. He clearly knew how to say the right words in the right order, and followed all the other instructions perfectly."

All of a sudden, Miss Sara looks up and says, "Isaac, what have you done?" She moans and wipes a tear from the corner of her eye.

Isaac, who's Isaac? I think. I look at Ziv, Noam and Ellah. They all shrug.

"Who's Isaac?" I ask softly.

"Isaac is my brother."

"I thought his name was Lavan," I say.

"Oh, Lavan, that's a name he made up for himself after our mother was murdered."

We all gasp. Ellah rushes over to Miss Sara and takes her hand.

"It's such a long story." Miss Sara sighs, and lowers her head to her desk.

We all sit as still as statues, hardly breathing.

Ellah pats her shoulder and says, "We need to know about your brother because we're the only ones who know what he created. Please tell us."

Miss Sara raises her head and sits up straight. She swivels around in her chair and stares outside at the green pasture. A sheep bleats and we all jump. After a moment she turns back and, in a low voice, begins to tell her story.

"Many years ago," are her first words, and as I listen, I feel like she's beginning a fairy tale.

"I lived at home with my three sisters and my brother, Isaac. We had a small farm in a community near Haifa. My father grew grapes."

"He grew grapes? Did you make wine?" Noam asks.

"We did make a small vintage, but we didn't jump on the grapes or anything."

Noam's eyes sparkle.

"My father also spent his time studying Kabbalah and other ancient wisdom with my brother Isaac. He was the youngest. He was very bright and my father delighted in learning with him."

"It's always the boys who get to study with their fathers," Ellah says. "It's not fair."

I glance at her. She's frowning.

"It doesn't seem fair, does it?" Miss Sara says with a sigh. "Did your mother study with you?"

"Yes, she did, every day until the day she boarded the bus for Haifa to do some shopping." Miss Sara continues almost in a whisper. "On that day a terrorist exploded a car bomb and blew up the bus she was on."

We gasp. We've all been warned about terrorist attacks but we never knew anyone who was killed in one.

Miss Sara rocks back and forth in her chair for a moment. Then she continues. "Isaac was riding his bike along the road when it happened. All he could talk about for months afterwards was the black twisted form of the bus; the smoke rising and the people screaming." Miss Sara gulps and swipes at her eyes. "That was the last time we ever saw her."

The room is silent. I sniff loudly. I can almost smell the burning bus in my nostrils. I get up from my seat.

"Don't you want to hear the rest?" Ziv asks me.

I mutter something noncommittal but I sit back down.

"Isaac was very close to our mother, and her death and what he saw pained him deeply. He dropped out of school. Day and night he studied ancient texts. I think he believed he could make a golem like our mother and bring her back, or something." Miss Sara shakes her head.

"If he could do that he'd really be famous," Ellah says.

"I don't think he wanted to be famous. He just wanted our mother back."

Ellah nods. Her face is full of sympathy.

"Then he and my father began quarreling all the time. Isaac left the house and moved into the small shed behind the vines, with all of the books my father had about golems. He claimed it was quieter out there. A few days later he told us he'd changed his name. 'I'm not Isaac anymore,' he said. 'Isaac's dead. I'm Lavan.'"

"Where did he get that name from?" Ziv asks.

It's a name he chose to honor our mother, whose name was Levana, which means moon. Did you ever know someone really well who's changed his name?" Miss Sara asks us.

We all shake our heads.

"It's really hard to remember to call someone a name that you're not used to. Anyway, one night my father found him in the woods, singing and praying, with the golem book in front of him. My father was shocked. "

"So what happened?" Ellah asks.

"My father forbade him to ever create a golem."

"Ouch," Ziv groans.

"My brother packed up his things and disappeared. From time to time I hear reports about him from people who still see him."

Sadness hangs in the room like fog.

"Every time something strange happens in Kfar Keshet people say Lavan did it." Ellah turns to us.

"Everyone knows that Lavan practices magic and that he created snakes with legs and trees with ears," I say.

"You've heard about snakes with legs?" Miss Sara asks. "I thought that was a secret."

"Oops." I cover my mouth with my hand.

"Tell me," Miss Sara commands.

I swallow to clear the lump in my throat and say, "Mom and Dad told me that one time Lavan created snakes with legs and they attacked Kfar Keshet."

Miss Sara exhales a deep breath. "We were trying to keep that a secret from you kids," she whispers. "Who else knows about this incident?"

Noam raises his hand. Ellah and Ziv just look blank. "Tell me," Ziv says. "I hate to be the one who doesn't know a secret."

Miss Sara swivels in her chair and points to a large, weighty bow and arrow that hang on her office wall. I've seen it a million times but I've never asked her about it.

"Mr. Freed used that bow and arrow ten years ago when Lavan, with his magic, created magical snakes. We weren't sure what they wanted, but the only place they attacked was the school and the kindergarten building. Somehow Lavan knew about your special gifts. I guess he wanted to stop you from becoming special."

Our mouths fall open and it seems to me that the air in the room turns dry. I'm thinking that Mr. Freed doesn't look strong enough to pull that bow.

"Ten years ago, before his heart attack, Mr. Freed was in top physical shape," Miss Sara says, as though reading my mind. "He used to practice shooting with that bow all the time."

"Why didn't he just use a gun?" Noam wants to know.

"Mr. Freed discovered that guns can't kill Lavan's creations because they're magic."

"Oh, boy, this is really exciting." Ziv rubs his hands together.

"Lavan must have been perfecting his knowledge of Kabbalah and magic," Miss Sara begins. "One morning, we saw three black and grey snakes popping out of the grass here at Kfar Keshet. They were shrieking, a high-pitched shrill. They had legs. When snakes move on their bellies they aren't that fast, but these snakes with legs were able to run and jump everywhere. They were large, and the scales on their backs formed the letter 'L'."

Somewhere in the back of my mind is a slight recollection of a snake running through the grass. I feel the hair on the back of my neck stand up. "Why did he send snakes?" I ask.

"I'm not sure," Miss Sara says. "They moved really quickly, and the noise they made stopped everything. Maybe Lavan didn't think we could protect you kids."

Ziv bounces around in his chair. "What happened?" he asks, trying to speed the story along.

"At first no one knew what to do. Your nursery school teachers boarded the doors and windows. They could hear the snakes crawling over the walls, looking for a way in. It was terrible."

The shock makes me shake all over.

"Did the snakes harm anyone?" Ellah asks.

Miss Sara turns for a minute in her chair and then turns back. She is squeezing her knuckles and they are bright red. I sit forward in my chair, eager for her answer. She clears her throat and says, "It's unclear what Lavan was doing. The sound was impossible to listen to and we knew it would have some affect on you kids, but we weren't sure what. We all walked around and held our ears. We knew we had to get rid of the snakes."

"Is that when Mr. Freed saved us?" I ask.

"Yes," Miss Sara says as she glances again at the bow and arrow. "It was an emergency. I had been working with two boys who were trying to understand their gifts. Somehow the sound the snakes were making interfered with the process. They never were able to find out what their gifts were. One I had named Or, because he was supposed to have a gift related to light, and the other was Adam, who should have had a gift connected with the earth. Neither of them ever discovered their gifts."

I shudder. I hope that's not the reason I haven't learned my gift yet.

"Somehow Lavan was able to create snakes with a particular tonal quality. A tone that could completely wipe out the gifts."

We all gasp.

"We called for Mr. Freed to come at once. He arrived clutching his revolver. He shot at them but they didn't die. He ran home and grabbed his bow and arrow. Then he tracked down the largest snake of the three, who seemed to be their leader. It was on the roof of the nursery school, about to slide down the chimney. Mr. Freed climbed into the tree opposite the nursery school, and waved his arms and yelled to make himself a target for the snake. It didn't work. The snake ignored him and continued to scale up the chimney. Mr. Freed raised his bow and shot an arrow through the neck of the snake, between its head and its first row of legs."

Miss Sara points to her neck to show us. Then she says," The snake fell from the roof, so Mr. Freed saw that the wooden arrow had succeeded where bullets had failed. The other two snakes surrounded the fallen snake, as though to keep it safe. Mr. Freed raised his bow again and shot each of them. The arrows went through the snakes and buried themselves in the ground. The snakes were pinned to the earth. "

Silence fills the room. We are mesmerized.

"And then?" Ziv prompts.

"And then, Mr. Handler, the village gardener, stepped forward with a shovel. He struck the two smaller snakes with all of his might and severed their heads."

"Yuck!" Ellah says. "How disgusting. I never heard that before."

"What happened to the boss snake? I hope he died too," I say.

"Unfortunately, he managed to slither away."

"With an arrow in him? How?"

"Maybe it was because he wasn't a natural snake, but magical. Mr. Freed and Mr. Handler chased after him. At the lake in the woods, the same place you saw Lavan create the golem, they caught up with the snake, and as Mr. Freed raised his bow, he thought he saw Lavan staring at him from behind the trees. Mr. Freed shot his arrow directly into the snake's head. At that moment he saw Lavan slump to the ground. That's how we first understood that Lavan was behind the attack and realized what Lavan had become. What was interesting was that the death of the snake somehow affected Lavan's health."

We all gasp.

"Snakes, golems . . . what else can he create?" I asked.

"Well, my brother had another interest beside golems. My mother was a doctor, and Isaac read all of her books about cloning. Just think, if he created his own people and educated them himself all of them would think like him. Then he would have a world where people wouldn't upset the peace because they would all be alike. Differences in people is what upsets him."

"But could he really do that?" Ellah asks.

"I don't think they're cloning people yet. But if my brother can change snakes and create golems he might have learned enough magic to clone people. He's clearly a very dangerous man."

My heart skips a beat. "We have to think about what we're going to do. This golem is a danger to Kfar Keshet."

"We can only guess why Lavan created him and sent him here," Miss Sara says. "But we know he is programmed to do whatever Lavan tells him to do. It follows that the only way we can defeat Lavan is to destroy the golem." She looks at each of us.

"How does that defeat Lavan?" Ziv wants to know.

"Well, I would expect that just like with the snakes, some of Lavan's energy is also in the golem. Think of Geppetto, who created Pinocchio. All of the energy he put into creating his puppet. Pinocchio was like a son to him. Wouldn't he lose energy if something happened to Pinocchio?"

"Are you saying Pinocchio was like a golem?"

Miss Sara nods.

I'm blown away.

"If we defeat the golem it should cause Lavan to lose some of his strength."

I'm about to ask Miss Sara if the golem is living off of Lavan's energy when Ziv asks, "Why does he want to rule the world?"

"Because even as a teenager he believed he was the only one who had found a way to bring peace to the world. My mother always said 'peacefulness was next to godliness'. I think Lavan misunderstood her words. I think he believes if he brings peace to the world he will be godly."

My mouth falls open. "You mean he thinks he'll be God?"

"He doesn't think he'll be God, but he will have some godly attributes. He has one already; he is a creator."

I look at my friends. Their eyes are wide open, like giant sunflowers. We're all in shock.

Miss Sara clears her throat and asks, "If the golem comes to the village, will you recognize him?"

We look at each other.

"I . . . I don't think I would," Ziv mutters.

"I'm not sure I would either. There was a full moon, but it was pretty misty," I say.

The others agree.

"I have no idea what this golem is being instructed to do, but whatever it is, it won't be for the good of the village. We have to be very careful." Miss Sara pauses, thinking for a moment. "A golem usually has a word written on his forehead. Did you see a word on his forehead?"

We all shake our heads.

"If you see a stranger with something on his forehead it

could be the golem. You're the only ones who know about the golem. This must be kept secret. It would just scare everyone."

We nod and agree to keep it a secret, even from our parents.

More nervous than before we arrived, we file out of Miss Sara's study and head home.

Chapter 8

My Treasure Box

THE morning after our meeting with Miss Sara, I sit at the kitchen table pushing the eggs around my plate like a robot. The house is quiet. Ziv stayed over at Noam's house last night. Ima's in her study working on her illustrations for picture books. Abba is plowing the left field with the tractor. I drum my fingers on the table and stare off into the distance. When I take a bite out of my toasted bagel it's tasteless. I plunk it down with a thud and carry my plate to the sink. I know what I have to do.

Out in the front yard, I study the house. All is quiet. My heart is beating like an over wound clock. I haven't seen my secret treasure chest in a long time. I climb the large cedar tree in our front yard and brace myself against a wide limb. I reach into the hole where two large branches cross over each other. The rough bark scratches my hand.

I lift the small wooden box out of its hiding place and I raise the lid. I always feel a tickle in my throat when I look in my box. Inside is a gray air force beret. Under it is a white plastic airplane with F-15 printed in blue on the wings, a small plastic Superman action figure, and an air force insignia pin.

I seat Superman on one of the branches. Then I fly the

miniature plane around and through the leaves in front of me. Flying the plane always helps me think. After a few minutes I begin to carefully replace my flying treasures back in the box.

"Hey, Jordan," Ziv yells from below. "Getting ready to fall out of that tree?"

My body jerks. I grab for a branch. My hand knocks Superman and he falls to the ground.

Ziv giggles. "Oh, now it's Superman who's falling out of trees."

"What's Superman doing in that tree?"

It's Ellah's voice. My face turns hot. I know it's beet red. I look between the branches. Noam, Ziv, and Ellah are all standing below, looking up at me.

"None of your business," I say through gritted teeth. "Go away."

"Sure thing," Ziv says. He bends down and picks up the Superman and waves it at me. "See you around." The three start heading toward the house.

"Wait," I shout. "I'm coming down." I shove the box under my shirt and slide down the tree trunk.

"What's that bump in your shirt? Is it from falling out of a tree?" Ziv asks with a smirk.

"Nah, it's . . . it's a box." My cheeks are still burning.

Ziv's eyes light up. Everyone steps forward for a closer look. I resist for a second, but they're my friends. So, I pull the box out from under my shirt. It's actually a relief to show it to them.

"What an awesome box," Ellah says.

"What's inside?" Ziv wants to know.

"It's my collection."

"You have a collection? What are you collecting?" Ellah asks.

"All kinds of things."

"Can we see?" Ziv hops up and down with excitement.

I can't decide. A treasure box at my age? I'm embarrassed. It's been a secret for so long. I look at my friends. They're waiting.

I finally say, "Before I show you my treasure box you've got to take the secret oath. No one else can know what's in this box."

"Sure," Ziv says. "I'm great with secrets."

Ziv actually is good with secrets. Most of the time.

Noam and Ellah nod, too.

I face them. They have solemn looks on their faces. I raise my right hand. "Repeat after me: 'Aleph, aleph, beit, beit, keep this secret and never forget.' "

My friends repeat the oath that Ziv and I made up years ago using the first two letters of the Hebrew alphabet.

Solemnly, they each raise their right hand and repeat the oath.

Then I start to open the box. At that moment I hear a rustling sound. I stuff the box inside my shirt. "Ima's coming," I whisper.

"No, I think it's a rabbit," Ziv whispers back.

I look over my shoulder and wait a second longer. It's nothing. All clear. I pull the box out from under my shirt and open it.

Ziv's eyes flash with delight. He reaches into the box and fingers my treasures.

"These make you think about flying," Ellah whispers.

"I know. That's why I collected them."

"They're great," Noam says.

"You've got to get rid of them. They're not water things," Ziv remarks.

"They're neat," Ellah says.

"Miss Sara told Jordan his gift has to do with water, not flying," Ziv responds.

"So why does he have to get rid of them?" Noam asks.

"Because he's not supposed to think about flying. He's

supposed to think about water. If he's always playing and thinking about flying he might never get his gift," Ziv says.

Noam and Ellah gasp.

Red heat creeps up my neck. Ziv is telling my friends everything. I want to kill him.

I lean against the trunk of the tree, touching the lid of my treasure box.

This is my collection. Now I have to get rid of it? What if I still don't get my gift? I'd have thrown away my box for nothing.

"You're almost thirteen," Ziv says, and crosses his arms.

"I know." I bite my lip.

"We could have a little ceremony to say good-bye to your collection," Ellah says. "Would that make it easier?"

I nod slowly, and then an exciting thought pops into my head. "I've got it. We'll throw them over the dam."

"The dam?" Ellah inhales sharply.

"It's dangerous," Noam says.

"It's against the law to go up there," Ziv adds.

I swallow hard. "Don't worry. We'll be okay."

There's nothing to be afraid of, I'm thinking. We've all been to the top of the dam with our teachers. It's pretty up there. No one's ever gotten hurt.

And anyways, having my treasures fly into the water is the perfect send-off.

Chapter 9

The Treasure Box Ceremony

"IT'S going to be fine," I tell my friends for the hundredth time. "No one's going to see us. We'll do it really fast and we'll be back at the lake in no time."

We leave the house. My treasure box is nestled in my arms. It's as unknowing as a little calf about to be sacrificed. Ziv is wearing his backpack to carry the things we're going to need for the ceremony.

We take a shortcut through the hip-high dry grass in the direction of the hydroelectric dam. The grass swishes as we make our way through. Bright sunlight beams feel hot on our heads. The happy voices of the kids splashing in the lake above the dam seem to be calling us to join them.

As we approach the dam, Noam and Ellah start walking slower and slower.

"Come on. You guys are holding us up," I say. I'm all jumpy, like a wound-up toy.

"Let's go swimming and leave this for tomorrow," Noam says. "There'll be time tomorrow."

I shake my head. "I can't wait another day to find out my gift. What if the golem comes?"

Ziv, Noam, and Ellah exchange doubtful looks.

"You said you would help me. First the ceremony, then a swim. Okay?" I say to Noam.

Noam bites his fingernail but finally nods.

We're almost at the dusty footpath. The tramp of curious villagers' feet has worn it into the ground over the years.

We pass the large red sign with big black letters that says: "STAY OUT."

The dam is right in front of us. We see the forty meter concrete span that stretches between the two sides of the river.

"Hold it," Noam says in a funny voice. "This is too dangerous. I'm not going any farther."

Ellah nods.

"You two are going to chicken out? It's not so dangerous," I use my confident voice.

"Did you see that sign? It says 'Stay Out'." Noam's voice sounds squeaky.

"Let's throw the things into the lake. It doesn't need to be over the dam," Ellah says.

"No way," I say. "We've got to fly them. They need the height."

"I'm not going any farther," Noam says. He turns around and starts walking back down the narrow path.

"It's too scary for me," Ellah says. "See you at the lake when you're through." She follows Noam.

I'm pissed. My two best friends are scaredy-cats. Ziv stands waiting behind me. His usually pink cheeks are chalky-white.

"It's okay," I say, and stand up straighter. "We'll be done in a few minutes."

Ziv stares at me. His eyes are wide open and he is biting his lower lip.

"Let's do it. We can't stand here forever." I move forward toward the dam.

"I'm only doing this to help you find your gift," Ziv says. "I'm really nervous."

"It's not so dangerous." I have to shout to be heard over the thundering sound of the water sluicing through the dam. The noise almost drowns out my voice. Even I can barely hear it.

At the edge of the dam, Ziv drops his backpack and removes the red cloths we packed. We tie them around our necks like two red-caped superheroes. It's for the ceremony. We inch our way across the narrow path toward the top of the massive concrete dam. It's about a meter wide. Step by step we move forward to the middle of the huge retaining wall. From the top of the wall, we look down about a million meters to where we can see the water rushing out the bottom of the dam into the Jordan with a deafening roar.

Ziv stares at the whooshing water as if hypnotized and groans. "Standing makes me dizzy," he shouts over the dam's pounding waterfall. He sits down, his feet dangling off the edge facing the waterfall and the river beyond.

"Open the box and do it fast so we can get down from here."

I flip open the cover of my treasure box. My heart hammers in my chest. I take out the beret and rub its softness up and down my leg. Will the air force arrest me if I throw the beret over the dam?

"Well?" Ziv shouts.

I sit down next to Ziv on the dam and continue rubbing the beret on my leg.

Ziv begins to whistle loud enough for me to hear over the roar of the dam.

"You know I hate when you whistle." I frown at him.

"Tough!" Ziv yells. "I hate watching you rub that stupid beret. Just let it go. Shoot it off. Do it!"

I roll the beret into a tight wad and fling it over the dam. The beret spreads like a parachute as it floats down. Far below we dimly see the current snatch the beret and it whirls down the river.

"Are you okay?" Ziv asks.

It's nice of Ziv to ask, but I don't say anything. I pick out

Superman next. I lean forward and put the small super-hero on the ledge. I whack it. Superman tumbles forward and dives headfirst into the water.

Then I lift out the toy airplane. I push it along the concrete as though it's taking off. Then I throw it way up into the sky. An air current catches the plane and it floats out over the dam as though it's flying.

"Would you look at that!" Ziv yells.

We're both surprised.

"It's really flying," Ziv says. He scrambles to his feet, suddenly not afraid of the height.

My heart is bursting as I watch the toy plane. It can fly. Why can't I?

The plane noses down, heading for the river below. That's when it happens.

"Bummer," I hear Ziv say. "It's going to crash." Ziv leans over the lip of the concrete dam to try and see where the plane is going to end its flight.

"Get down from there, you punks!" It's the angry voice of a guard. Startled by the shout, Ziv steps backwards. His heel stomps hard on something. It crunches. I look down at my treasure box. It's broken. I look up as Ziv lurches forward, tottering on the edge of the dam. I scramble to grab his hand. He's too far away. His arms spin like a pinwheel. As I watch, my heart in my throat, Ziv hurls over the wall, his red cape flaring behind him like he's flying.

"Help!" Ziv yells again and again. His voice gets softer and softer. Down he falls into the churning water below.

I lean over the edge of the dam. The red cloth swirls in the rapids below. I'm frozen. The only thing working in my body is my furiously beating heart. Then my voice kicks in.

"Ziv, Ziv!" I scream over the thundering water. The only sound I hear is the guard yelling "mayday, mayday" over his radio.

I stand on the edge of the wall. Ziv has disappeared in the churning waters below.

My heart stops.

I killed my brother!

I kick off my shoes and dive in.

Chapter 10

Saving Ziv

'M flying.

I don't splash when I break through the churning waters – I flow.

The water swirls around me, full of bubbles, leaves, tiny pebbles, and microscopic creatures. As I sink, or float, or whatever I'm doing underwater, my vision is crystal clear. All I think about is Ziv. Finally I see him. His body is tumbling downstream through the relentless current.

I zoom forward, but I'm barely moving a muscle. It's like I'm a part of the water, and every small movement brings me closer to Ziv. There is no edge between the water and me.

I am water. No hands. No feet. Panicked thoughts rush through my head. How do I get Ziv out of here?

Caught in the roiling current, Ziv thrashes about. A strong current drags him below the surface. Then another one tosses him upward. He rises, coughing. The shock draws taut lines around his mouth.

I twirl around in the water. The twirl creates a whirlpool. It pulls Ziv toward me. I see his head bob to the surface. He splutters water out of his mouth. I've got to get his head up. I coax a bed of water under Ziv's body. I'm his pillow. Ziv's head and chest stay above the water. Ziv opens his frightened eyes and stops thrashing. He lifts his head and looks around. He's floating on a bed of water. He's safe. He lies back and lets the water carry him.

When we reach the shallows, Ziv bumps against the bank and crawls onto the river shore, coughing up water.

Undulating with the current, I watch him. My tears of relief disappear into the lapping water.

* * *

Ziv lies on his back, his arms flung out, his eyes shut. He fingers his chest, his neck. He has lost the red cape. His shirt is in shreds. He opens his eyes. His upper body is covered with puffy red welts from the churning debris. He winces when he touches them. His arms are covered with bloody scratches. His face is full of scratches, too. The little finger on his right hand is sticking out on a funny angle. It's swollen and purple. He sits up. He puts his head between his knees to take deep breaths. He sits dripping, shaking. His body looks all loose and jiggly.

As a large puddle of water, I ooze out of the rapids. A flash of sunlight sparkles on me. Sliding along the ground I feel all quivery. The ground keeps sticking to me like I'm jelly. Some parts of me start to feel like they're getting firmer.

Ziv blinks. I can see the hair on the back of his neck standing on end.

I try to call him and tell him it's okay. He's just staring. I congeal. I pile up into the air like a pillar. Looking down I see the lower half of my body split into an upside down V. The V forms into my legs. Vibrations rise from my legs, shaking my arms out of the pillar. My chest and head start to take shape. I'm no longer transparent water. Like boiling milk and cornstarch, I'm becoming more solid by the nano-second. Then I'm Jordan again.

I turn over my hands and stare at them. I look down at my feet and pat my dripping body. It's me, all right. I even see the little birthmark on my left leg.

I'm myself. I snap my fingers and rush over to where Ziv is sitting.

Ziv gasps and says weakly, "You found your gift. And you saved my life."

I nod. A huge grin splits my face.

Along the riverbank, uniformed men are running everywhere.

I grab Ziv by the arm. "Look!" I point to the men. They're searching for us." I brace Ziv against my shoulder and help him stand up.

One of the uniformed men spots us. Then they're all running alongside the river toward us.

"There you are," the guard says, huffing to catch his breath. He's the one who had shouted at us on the top of the dam. "We've been looking all over for you."

"Sorry, we didn't mean to cause any trouble," Ziv says weakly.

"Sorry?" the watchman says. "Our entire staff has been looking for you. We had to shut down the dam. You caused a blackout in three towns. It will take time to restart the dam."

When the watchman stops speaking I realize that the river no longer sounds like it's rushing along. That must be what happens when the dam is turned off.

My face turns scarlet. "It was my idea. We were only doing a little ceremony."

"I didn't know I was going to fall in," Ziv says.

More uniformed men gather around us. "Did you hear that?" the watchman jeers. "They were only doing a little ceremony. They didn't know they were going to fall in. Just like kids nowadays. No respect for the rules."

"He only meant . . ." Ziv starts to explain. Then we hear a familiar voice.

"Jordan! Ziv!" Ima is standing before us all frantic and wild-eyed. She's breathing heavily. She must have run all the way from home. She hugs us hard. "I was so worried. Ellah and Noam came to the house to tell me you were doing something dangerous on the dam," she says, tears tumbling down her cheeks. "What were you thinking?"

"Listen, ma'am," the guard begins politely. "We've posted signs all along that path to keep people from climbing up to the dam. Your sons were on the top of the dam itself, in complete disregard of the rules."

Ima's ears turn ruby red. She's angry. She turns to us. I tremble under her angry stare. Ziv's lower lip quivers.

"What's got into you?" she yells. Without waiting for an answer she continues. "You were taught to follow the rules. I can't believe this. I'm so ashamed."

I look at the ground. Ziv swipes at the tears running down his cheeks.

"And look at you Ziv. You're all cut up and bleeding. You need first-aid." She turns to the guard. "I've got to get my son to the hospital."

In less than a minute, we hear the sound of an ambulance approaching. The driver guides the ambulance over the grass and gets as close to the river as he can. Two paramedics jump out of the back of the ambulance and run towards us. One of them is carrying a stretcher.

"I can walk," Ziv keeps saying.

"Not in your condition, buddy," one of the paramedics says.

They lay the stretcher on the ground and gently place Ziv on it. Then they lift it up and carry Ziv to the open door of the ambulance.

Ima grabs my arm and we stumble towards the waiting vehicle together. I climb inside as the paramedic helps Ima in. We sit down opposite the gurney that Ziv is lying on,

and the ambulance bumps and grinds away from the riverbank to the road.

"Ima!" I say as we travel along.

"Not now Jordan!"

"But Ima, my gift—"

"Jordan saved my life!" Ziv tries to tell her.

"I'm water!" I say at the same time.

"Water . . . ?" Ima turns her confused and angry face
toward us. It's a funny expression, but I don't feel like
laughing.

"He did it, Ima, he—" Ziv says.

I lean toward Ziv, interrupting him, and whisper. "Let it
go. We'll tell her later."

"But it's your big moment. She should be so proud of
you," he whispers back.

My shoulders sag. Was that really my gift? Will I know
how to do it again? I stare blindly out the ambulance window. Am I a hero or a troublemaker? I don't know what to
think.

Chapter 11

Miss Sara Gets the Scoop

AS we approach the hospital, Ima looks at us and says
sternly, "Just wait until Abba hears about this."
I shudder. It's all my fault. Who knew Ziv would fall
in? It seemed so safe to me.

The ambulance drops the three of us off at the entrance
to the emergency room. Ziv, Ima, and I enter the cool,
white-walled hospital. I sneeze three times. It has something to do with that hospital odor. The smell of the sterile
cleaners and alcohol tickle my nose.

Ziv moans as he sits down in a brown plastic chair. I go
to the water dispenser and bring back three plastic cups of
water for us.

Finally the head nurse, Nurse Emunah, arrives. She
looks like a storybook nurse in her bright snowy-white uniform. "What happened to you?" she asks Ziv.

He just groans.

"My, oh my." The nurse peels off Ziv's ragged shirt.
"You've had some swim today. Are you the guys responsible for the power shortage we just had?"

My cheeks flush again. I lower my gaze and stare at my
bare feet.

"We were in the middle of X-raying a broken leg and

all of the electricity went off. Can you imagine? At least it was a good way to test our new generator. It worked like a charm." Nurse Emunah inspects Ziv's little finger.

"This looks like a break," she says calmly.

Ziv whimpers.

"Nurse Emunah, is he okay?" a new voice asks.

Everyone looks up. Miss Sara has entered the emergency room.

"How did you find out?" Ima asks, wide-eyed.

"When the dam stops running, I'm the first to know in our town," she replies.

She examines Ziv's scraped, welted body. "I guess I don't have to go any further to find out who caused the power outage."

Ziv begins to sniffle. I open my mouth to explain, but the words stick in my throat.

Miss Sara stands by Nurse Emunah and asks, "How serious are his injuries?"

"He'll be fine." We all smile. "These cuts and bruises will heal fairly quickly, but his finger is definitely broken. I'm going to splint his finger and spread a healing aloe cream over all of these contusions. They look worse than they are," Nurse Emunah says. "Excuse us now," she says to Miss Sara, looking at me sternly but saying nothing else. She takes Ziv and our mother with her to a treatment room.

I look at the floor, and then up at Miss Sara. I'm relieved she's here. There is a tickle of excitement in my stomach. I try to control myself for Ziv's sake, but I'm sure Miss Sara is going to be delighted with what I've discovered.

"I did it. I did it." My words bubble out. "I didn't mean to knock out the power. I saved Ziv's life and found my gift. It was amazing."

Miss Sara shakes my hand. "That's great news," she says calmly.

I punch the air and dance a little jig.

Miss Sara smiles at my excitement.

"Come with me," she says abruptly. I follow her down the white-tiled hall to a brown wooden door. Miss Sara enters the room. The square room has a wooden desk piled high with papers and a small sofa. She points to the sofa and I sit down, but a moment later I'm up again, prancing around the room.

"It was so amazing and unbelievable." I'm jumping from one foot to the other. "I found my gift. Now I know. It's not flying. I was there in the water. It was like I *was* the water. Then I was saving Ziv and then rolling onto the bank and becoming me. It was great." The words pour out of my mouth like water gushing out of the dam.

"Jordan, you are so lucky to have found your gift, but couldn't you have done it in a different way? Shutting down the dam caused a blackout in three towns."

I look at her, all hot faced, but Miss Sara doesn't sound angry or annoyed. I look up at the ceiling to calm down. In a moment I feel better.

I move my arms like I'm swimming. "I didn't think we'd do anything bad by going up to the dam. I needed to fly my collection. We were going to be up there for five minutes. That's all."

"You ignored the "Keep Out" sign."

My face turns hot again. I stare at the floor. We did disobey, but villagers go up there all the time. I don't say that, though. I know it's no excuse. I stand silently.

"Go on," Miss Sara says softly.

I'm silent for a few more moments. How could I have done such a dumb thing? I could have killed my brother. Tears build up behind my eyes.

"It was a dramatic way to find your gift," Miss Sara's gentle voice fills the silence. "I'm curious to know what happened."

I look into her smiling face, take a big gulp of air, and

continue my story. "I didn't know when I jumped into the water that I would become water. I just wanted to save Ziv. I didn't even know how, but he's my brother . . ."

She nods, understanding in her eyes.

"It's funny, you know. I'm kinda nervous. Maybe I won't be able to do it again."

"Don't worry. No one has a gift just one time. You'll do it again. I'm sure."

I sit down on the couch next to her and exhale like an accordion releasing a note.

"Another strange thing happened, Miss Sara. I don't think I had my clothes on in the water, but when I reconstructed, or whatever you want to call it, they were on me."

"I know," Miss Sara says. "It's part of your gift." Miss Sara sits quietly for several minutes, staring off into space.

I squirm on the sofa.

Then she looks at me again, and it's like her eyes are staring right through me. The hair on the back of my neck feels all prickly.

"Jordan, there are a set of rules that come with each gift. Are you ready to hear your rules? First . . ."

I look around the office. Miss Sara is right next to me but her voice sounds like it's coming from outer space. I think I hear a loud school bell ringing in my ears. What did she say? I cover my ears.

"I said, 'First of all . . .'"

Her voice fades away again. I feel spooked.

Then Miss Sara snaps her fingers at me like I'm not paying attention. She points to her mouth. I look at her mouth. She's speaking but I can't hear the words. My scalp prickles all over. I try to speak. Nothing. I clear my throat. I strain to hear Miss Sara's words. Suddenly Miss Sara's voice sounds clear again. I hear the end of her sentence: ". . . not to play games or show off."

She looks at me sternly.

"You're having the usual problem," Miss Sara says. "New gift receivers are too wired to listen. I'll begin again." This is really weird.

"Thank you," I say.

Miss Sara's calm voice begins again. This time I can hear her. "First of all, Jordan, your gift is a precious thing. It must only be used to help people in trouble, exactly the way you helped Ziv today. When you become like water you will be able to do all kinds of things. You'll be able to flow under locked doors and into sealed-off places. You'll be able to hold people up in the water and save them from drowning like you did today. You'll be able to gather up your energy and make a tsunami wave to defeat your enemy."

"Yes! Wow!" I jump up. "I'm the water man." I sway my hands and hips like I'm swimming.

Miss Sara pats the sofa and I sit down again. I make a serious face so Miss Sara will know that I'm paying attention.

"As you get older and more comfortable with your gift, you will find all kinds of uses for it," Miss Sara continues. "But always remember, these gifts are there to help people in trouble, and not for playing games or showing off."

I'm hypnotized by Miss Sara's eyes. I feel comfortable and strange at the same time.

Miss Sara taps a finger on the table to get my attention. I blink.

"Jordan, you've become one of the gifted children of Kfar Keshet. Our community is based on the principle that all children can be special as long as we adults don't discourage them."

I know the principles of Kfar Keshet. I nod politely. I've heard this.

"There are people in the world who are afraid of the children of Kfar Keshet."

I laugh. "Afraid of me?"

Miss Sara hesitates for a second and then speaks. "They're afraid of any child who is different from the others."

"Really afraid of us?"

"Yes. The people who are really scared of you, and children like you, want to normalize you."

"Normalize?" My eyebrows shoot up. "You mean like take away my powers?"

"Yes."

"No! I just found my powers. I don't want to be normal." I jump to my feet and ball my hands into fists.

"I know, Jordan. You know about my brother . . ."

She pats the sofa.

I sit beside her again. "Lavan, your brother. Yeah. You told us about him the other day."

"I told you he wants to control the world and get rid of kids like you. He knows that because of your special gifts you have the ability to defeat him. You can appear from unexpected places, Noam can manipulate clouds, Eden can create from her dreams. Even with all of Lavan's powers, he will never be able to control yours." Miss Sara smiles.

Wow, with our gifts we can stop Lavan! That's mind-boggling. Thinking about Lavan and the golem makes my throat feel like it's filled with pieces of tape that are trying to pull together.

Miss Sara smoothes her skirt and continues. "As you know, I named our village after the rainbow. When white light is seen through a prism it turns into lots of colors and makes a rainbow."

I nod, remembering the sixth grade experiments we did with light and prisms.

"You know, before Lavan left us he often talked about his world view. He believed if people were all the same you could end wars and make the world a peaceful place to live."

"Why do people have to be the same?" I ask.

"He believes that differences in people are what they fight about. If everyone was the same, people wouldn't fight over land, and religion, and ideas. They'd all agree with each other and understand each other."

"Does he think we'd all be speaking the same language?" I ask. "I'm sure misunderstandings happen because not all people speak the same."

"I don't know about that," Miss Sara says. She looks deeply into my eyes. "I think the differences in people are like the colors of the rainbow. Different thoughts and ideas from different people advance the world and make life interesting. My brother wants the world to be filled with white light, no other colors; a world with no diversity. Everyone will think and act the same way. He will control their every thought and action."

I scratch my head. It kind of makes sense to me. No disagreements, everyone thinking and believing the same thing.

Miss Sara stares at me like she can read my mind.

"Jordan, would you like to think and do exactly the same things as Ziv?

You would always agree on everything. You would be like a robot."

I can see Miss Sara's point. The things I like and don't like about people are what make them interesting.

"If Lavan is the only thinker, his creations will do whatever he wants. You know what that means? He will rule the world."

"That's mind control," I say.

Miss Sara nods.

I feel a tight knot forming in my stomach. "How can he do that?"

"As you know, Lavan has learned the wisdom of the ancients. He has great powers. He has created the golem.

He'll try to destroy us. As I mentioned earlier, I think he might also be trying to clone people. Just think, if he can create enough clones, he will have his own army to regulate the daily lives of the people. A number of clones scattered among a population could really keep things under control . . . under his rule."

My mind swims with all of these possibilities. Cloning is a new idea. But if he created a golem he could probably create anything he wants.

"Will I be able to use my gift against him to keep the village safe?" I ask. "Do you think water can fight a monster?"

"I hope so," Miss Sara says.

"Jordan, where are you?" I hear Ima calling. She must be looking for me in the hallway.

"I'm in here, Ima," I yell through the closed door.

"You need to go now," Miss Sara says.

I stand up. My legs are all shaky and I feel wobbly. Miss Sara smiles sweetly and snaps her fingers. My ears ring for a moment and then I'm able to straighten up and step forward. "Thank you for my magic gift. I'm so happy to know what it is."

Miss Sara shakes my hand. "It is really wonderful," she says. "But remember: don't use this gift in any way except to help people, or you'll be in trouble."

"Don't worry, Miss Sara, I won't."

But what could possibly go wrong? I ask myself as I walk out the door with a bounce in my step.

Chapter 12

Back to School

FOR the first time since June, my alarm clock blasts me awake. It's the end of summer, a week after the dam incident. I groan and pull the covers over my head. Then I hear my door yanked open and Ziv's eager voice fills my room.

"First day of school! Hurray!"

I sit up and rub my eyes, frowning. "No more swimming. No more tree climbing. Just studying all the time." All I want to do is sink back into my dream. I had been catching silver fish at the lake.

Ziv ignores my black mood. "I can't wait to see my friends. It's going to be a great year. I'm going to be in fifth grade and you're in seventh grade. Isn't that great?"

I don't answer, and thankfully, Ziv stops battering me with his enthusiasm.

We dress quickly and go downstairs. In the kitchen Ima has prepared a special back-to-school breakfast. I guess she's forgiven us for our mess-up at the dam. Our plates are piled with plump pancakes. Each pancake has a happy face drawn with chocolate syrup. Tall, frosty glasses of orange juice sit alongside mugs of chocolate milk.

"Wow," Ziv says, his face shining. He sits down, grabs his fork, and digs in.

I pull my chair back from the table and plop down. I raise my fork and pick at the pancakes on my plate. *School, what a bummer*, I'm thinking.

As soon as Ziv finishes his pancakes and one of mine, Ima urges us to hurry.

"You guys better get going." She shoos us out.

We head out the front door and down the path.

"What happened to the summer?" I ask as I kick a mound of dirt to the side of the path.

"It really flew by." Ziv giggles. "Flew by . . . do you get it? You thought you could fly and—"

"Give me a break." My sense of humor is still asleep at home.

Fifteen minutes later we're at school. We all file into the auditorium for the "Welcome Back to School" announcements. My friends and I slap each other on the back and yell hello across the big hall. Teachers, standing around the room, are frowning at us. I see Miss Sara standing on the stage waiting. Finally we settle into our seats and quiet down. Ellah, Noam, Ziv, and I sit together in the middle of the crowd.

Miss Sara steps up to the podium and speaks into the microphone. "Welcome back from summer vacation. I hope you all had a good time."

There are cheers and applause.

"Good." Miss Sara smiles at us. "I have a surprise for you today. Remember Mr. Portaal, who was a teacher here three years ago?"

"Yes," a few students shout out. A few groan. Others laugh in response.

Miss Sara puts up her hands to quiet the kids. "He's just returned to us from the university and he will be your new principal."

Some students clap politely.

"And you remember Mr. Portaal's son, Nadav," she continues. Nadav rises from his chair, smiles, and waves like he's a candidate running for the Knesset, the Israeli parliament.

I sink down in my chair and turn to Noam. "As you know, that kid is trouble, with those dumb black eyes and that fake smile."

"Give him a chance," Ellah mutters. "His parents just separated. That's got to be really hard to take."

"Separated?" Ziv asks.

"Yeah, like they're not living together anymore," Noam whispers.

"Oh!" Ziv whispers back.

As the assembly ends, we all file out. Dark-eyed Nadav is moving in our direction.

"Watch out. He's coming this way," I whisper. I'm annoyed with myself for feeling afraid of him.

Before we can push through the mob, Nadav and his old pal Nitzan make their way to where we're standing by the exit, waiting to file out of the auditorium.

"How you doing, Jor?" Nadav asks. "Heard you had a flight over the dam." Nadav elbows Nitzan in the ribs. They laugh.

My stomach folds into a knot. I clench my fists. There's no way I'm going to tell Nadav that the flight over the dam gave me my gift.

He continues, "Must have been a real shocker. Felt in three towns."

"Pretty good, eh?" I say. I don't wait for his answer. I turn away from him and move toward the door.

"Well, see you losers around," I hear Nadav sneer.

"Yah," Nitzan sneers, too, and then they walk away.

"Don't waste your energy," Noam whispers into my ear. "Arguing with the principal's son is not the smartest thing to do on the first day of school."

At 3:00 p.m., the PA system plays the end-of-the-school-day song. Waves of students gush out of the school. Ziv, Noam, Ellah, and I are carried along.

"Where are you guys going?" Noam asks when Ziv and I turn left up the street leading to Eden's house.

"We're going to Eden's zoo. Jacob asked us if we wanted an after-school job cleaning out the cages," I answer.

"Ugh!" Ellah rolls her eyes. "I'm glad he didn't ask me. Those animals are all crazy. Give me a healthy spider any day."

"It's good money," I say.

Ziv nods his agreement.

"Have a good time. And shower before you come over," Noam says and waves good-bye.

When we get to Eden's house we knock on the door. Jacob, Eden's father, opens it and steps outside. "Thanks for coming," he says. "I'm really pleased you want to work at the zoo."

"We're all set to help," I say.

"Okay, just wait here a minute," Jacob says, and he re-enters the house.

We look across the street, waiting. The zoo is a mixed-up mangle of cages across the road from Eden's house, surrounded by a high wooden fence. The wild animals are at the back, in metal cages. Tamer animals are closer to the house, in bamboo cages. All of the cages contain the misshapen, strange, and scary animals that three-year-old Eden has dreamed up in her sleep. Every week or two, Jacob has to build new cages to hold Eden's creations.

Among the strange creatures are Aish, a fire-breathing dragon; three winged horses colored red, pink, and blue; a cheetah with the face of an ape; and a three-headed dog. There are also a few animals from storybooks: the lion from *The Jungle Book*, an elephant from *Babar*, and a couple of monsters from *Where the Wild Things Are.*

"How could such a cute baby dream up so many monsters?" everyone always asks. "And why did she receive her gift so early?"

Miss Sara says that it probably has something to do with the fact that Eden was supposed to be one of twins. But when she was born, her twin was dead. Miss Sara believes that the energies of the lifeless twin are in Eden and therefore she developed her gift much faster than other children. Miss Sara says it reminds her of Elvis Presley, whoever that is. I asked my mom about Elvis Presley. She told me he was a man who sang songs and twisted and turned like a crazy man when he was singing, and that his twin died at birth. Everyone said he had the energy of his twin.

Ima told us that Eden's parents, Jacob and Tamar, do try to control Eden's creativity. They went to Miss Sara for advice and she told them to be careful of what books they read to Eden before she goes to sleep. Miss Sara even arranges for volunteers to spend some evenings in Eden's room so her folks can get some sleep themselves.

Jacob and Tamar don't want strangers from outside of

the village to find out about Eden's amazing gift. They've posted "Keep Out" signs all over the wooden fence to help keep curious people away.

Jacob comes out of his house wearing heavy black leather boots. We follow him across the street. "You ought to consider wearing other shoes," he comments as he opens the gate to the first pen. We look down at our favorite sport shoes and then into the cages. Muck is everywhere. Our shoes squelch as we walk into the zoo.

"We're searching for a zoo or safari to buy the animals," Jacob explains while he rakes a cage.

As we step outside of the cage, a tall man with big arms and shoulders comes up the path. "Just in time," Jacob says to him. "Meet our new helpers."

The man is dressed in brown work pants, a blue tee shirt, and a brown baseball cap. He stares at us through small, squinty blue eyes.

"Jordan, Ziv, meet Mordechai." The muscular man steps forward and shakes my hand. I feel a shock wave move up my spine. The man looks strangely familiar. Where have I seen him before? I look over at Ziv. He has a puzzled look on his face. I know he's wondering the same thing.

Jacob interrupts our thoughts. "Follow me. I'll show you where we keep the equipment you'll be using."

We follow Jacob across the gravel into a small wooden shed he built in one corner of the zoo. It's filled with the shovels, rakes, and brooms we'll use for cleaning the cages.

"Over there—" Jacob points toward the opposite fence, "—are the bales of hay we lay down after the floors of the cages are clean. Now I'll show you how we deal with the animals."

A cold fist grips my stomach. I try to put on a brave face as I follow Jacob toward one of the cages.

"You have to coax them out into the holding pens," Jacob explains as he unlocks the cage of the three-headed dog.

"They're generally pretty easy to handle, but don't worry. Mordechai and I will be working right alongside you."

After two hours of hard work, we're exhausted. We leave Jacob's zoo and walk home slowly, slumped over. My arms ache.

"Pee-yew, you stink." Ziv holds his nose and glares at me.

"You don't exactly smell like roses either," I say in an exhausted voice. "I wish I could go down to the Jordan and jump in."

"We're grounded for one more week," Ziv reminds me.

I swallow hard, thinking about the punishment we received because of the dam affair. We've been grounded for two weeks. No swimming or any association with the lake, the Jordan river, or the dam.

"Hi, boys," Ima says as we drag through the door. "You two look exhausted and you smell like animals." She pinches her nose. "Go upstairs and shower."

After our showers we go downstairs to the kitchen. Ziv sits down at the dinner table and flips a piece of salmon on to his plate. Then he passes the platter to me.

"That zoo is really hard work!" I say as I take some salmon. "The monsters have to be moved out of their cages so we can go in and clean them."

"The animals are smelly. Their cages are worse," Ziv adds as he hands me the mashed potatoes. Ima smiles at me as I heap two scoops on to my plate.

"How often do they clean the cages?" Abba wants to know.

"Several times a week," I say.

"The three-headed dog didn't want to leave his cage. One of the heads was worried that someone would take his bone," Ziv says.

I laugh. "That dog is really funny."

"Pass the salad," Ziv says.

"Pass the salad, *please*," Ima scolds, reminding Ziv to use the magic word.

"What are they doing about Aish?" Abba asks. "I remember when he was just a miniature dragon. Eden's first creation. Jacob caught him and put him in their breadbox. He almost burnt down their house when he started blowing sparks from his nose."

"He's not a problem. He's fun," I insist. "Kids love to toss paper scraps into his cage and watch him set them on fire." Ziv and I laugh.

"Does Jacob have anyone else helping him?" Ima asks.

I feel a little fish swim around in my stomach. Ziv and I exchange looks. "Yeah, a workman named Mordechai," I finally say.

"That's nice," Ima says. "Another hand to help out."

For some reason I don't want to talk about Mordechai. I change the subject. "Eden created a whole bunch of elves after Tamar read her a story about Santa Claus. Jacob's never been able to catch them. They've disappeared into the woods. No one knows where they are," I say.

Abba shakes his head.

Ima brings up a tray of brownies from the counter and sets it on the table. "Eden really has a special gift."

"It's under control right now, but I don't know how they're going to keep it that way," Abba adds, putting down his coffee cup.

"We all have to watch out for her," Ima continues, as if finishing Abba's thoughts. "She's such a beauty with her brown silky curls and pudgy cheeks. Someone might steal her and force her to dream up things that they want."

I sit up with surprise. The little fish in my stomach does somersaults. "Could that really happen here in Kfar Keshet?"

Ima looks at Abba for one second, in that silent communication way, clears her throat, and says, "Of course not.

Eden is being watched very closely. It's nothing to worry about."

I know there's something they're not telling me, and I'm not sure I want to know what it is. Miss Sara has already warned us.

I have my gift now, so I can help. The nervous fish jumping in my stomach settles down slightly.

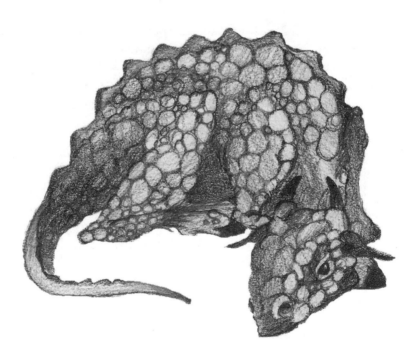

Chapter 13

Aish's Fire

"DO you smell something?" Ziv yells while I'm trying to coax the ape-cheetah back into his cage.

It's late the next day. School's out and we're back at the zoo.

I sniff deeply. It smells like something's burning. I hurriedly push the ape-cheetah back into his cage and carefully slide the lock into place.

Ziv runs over. There is a smell of scorched brush. "Look, over there." I point toward Mr. Goldman's wheat field where reddish-yellow flames are shooting up.

We race over there and see Aish, the fire-breathing dragon, standing in the middle of the wheat. He is aiming large bursts of fire at the dried wheat stalks in a corner of the field. He shoots a flame and then watches where it lands. He's having a great time.

"How did he get out?" I could swear we put Aish into the holding pen when we cleaned his cage. "Ring the fire bell," I yell as I run toward the dragon. And then I see that Eden is sitting next to Aish.

What's she doing? As I get closer I see her stand up and start toddling toward the fire. "Stop, Eden," I yell but she's too far away to hear me. Or she's not listening. She's moving closer and closer.

I'm water, I tell myself.

I need to do something but my head feels locked up.

Clang, clang! I hear the sound of the fire alarm bell, but looking around I see there's no one close enough to help. Then suddenly I see him – a large, muscled man wearing a blue baseball cap running from the upper pasture. Some kind of net is hanging from his hands. It could be Mordechai, but he doesn't move like him.

My arms break out in goose bumps. There's no time to think. The man and I are running at right angles to each other. I've got to get to Eden first. Maybe he's trying to kidnap her. My feet are racing. My arms are pumping. I'm flying toward Eden and the fire, but the man is gaining on me. My heart is nearly bursting as I force myself to go faster.

We need water . . . flowing water . . . Jordan River water . . .

Like a mantra, the words flow, blow, roll, fill my head.

One minute I'm a boy running through a field. Then suddenly I'm swirling along the ground, gushing through wheat plants, trickling over rocks, spreading over the land. I cascade onto the burning crops – water touching fire. Hissing sounds rise all around me.

I overflow and sweep Eden off her feet. She flounders in the water. I pillow her. The stranger runs forward, net outstretched to grab the toddler. I don't want him to touch Eden.

Force . . . water power . . . water force . . . the words tumble through my being.

Buffeting Eden, I gather force.

Splash!

A giant wave bowls the man off his feet. His hat falls off. I see his forehead. Is there something written on it? I roll past.

The man gets to his feet, water dripping from his hair.

He coughs and spits water from his mouth. His body is shaking from the force of the mini-tsunami wave I have become. He staggers back and forth. He bends down, grabs his hat, and pulls it down over his forehead.

A sudden rush of noise grabs my attention. The townspeople, screaming and carrying water buckets, are rushing toward Eden. Her father grabs her.

I whirl the water into an eddy and flow to the far side of the field. I feel pinpricks of pressure darting along the edges of my water. I quiver, look down, and realize that I'm standing upright, dripping wet. I turn around. The man in the baseball cap is gone.

Jacob and Eden are staring at me. I smile and wave.

"Where were you?" Jacob asks. "Why are you all wet?"

I shrug my shoulders. I am not sure if I should tell Jacob about my gift.

Chapter 14

Jacob Is Mad

"HOW in the world did Aish get out?" Jacob yells. "We have all kinds of rules to keep the animals in their cages. What happened?"

Mordechai, Ziv, and I are standing in a half circle facing Jacob. We're all busy digging holes in the dirt with the tips of our shoes. When I look up, I see Jacob's face and ears are beet red and sweat is running down his forehead.

There's a moment of silence and then I speak up. "Right before we smelled the fire, I was cleaning the ape-cheetah's cage," I stutter.

Ziv rubs the tip of his shoe back and forth in the dirt. I can see doubt winding its way through his head. He must be wondering if he locked the cage.

I had called him frantically to help me return the ape-cheetah to its cage. I was having trouble with the lunatic animal and he had rushed from the dragon's pen to help me.

"Ziv always closes and locks all of the cages. It couldn't have been him," I say.

Jacob looks at Ziv, "Well?"

Ziv shrugs. "I . . . I'm pretty sure I locked the cage . . . I'm pretty careful," he says slowly.

Mordechai stares at us. In his slow, heavy voice he says, "Ziv, do you remember when you were cleaning Aish's cage and I was feeding him? I heard Jordan call for help. Did you run out first?" His blue hat is pulled low over his forehead. He stands with his arms folded across his chest. "I thought I closed the gate, but I'm not a hundred percent sure, either."

I look from one to the other. Who blew it?

"I guess that means I was responsible," Mordechai says slowly.

"No . . ." Ziv starts to say, but everyone ignores him.

"This is really serious, Mordechai," Jacob says. "I know you need the money, but I think you should take a couple of days off until we get to the bottom of this."

Mordechai touches his hat to show that he understands what Jacob said, turns on his heels, and lumbers away.

"Maybe I wasn't so careful," Ziv begins to say, but Jacob is already moving toward his house.

I start toward Jacob to explain, but Ziv grabs my arm and pulls me to a stop. I see tears in his eyes.

"Let it go," he says.

We finish cleaning out the cages of the pastel-colored horses without speaking to each other. When we finish all the chores, we take the rakes and shovels back to the wooden shed and hang them up. We peel off our work gloves and, without saying good-bye to Jacob, start for home.

"I've got to speak to Miss Sara," I say, breaking the silence. "I think Mordechai has something on his forehead. I must tell her."

When we reach the end of the street, Ziv heads home and I continue on toward Miss Sara's house.

"Come in! I'm in the kitchen," Miss Sara shouts when I knock at her door. I push open the door and make my way to the kitchen. Miss Sara is washing dishes at the sink, wearing a yellow and green plaid apron over her dress.

"Jordan, how nice to see you," she says as she looks up. Her hands are all soapy. "Is everything okay?"

I pull out one of the kitchen chairs and slump down. "I think I did a bad thing today," I say in a low voice. Words spill out of my mouth like water through an open faucet. "I was helping Jacob with the animals and I was having trouble with the ape-cheetah. Ziv ran over to help me and maybe he didn't lock the dragon's cage correctly. Aish got out and started a fire in Mr. Goldman's field. I became a wave and knocked over Mordechai, or someone who looked like Mordechai, who was trying to grab Eden and his hat fell off and he has something on his forehead and then—"

Miss Sara puts up a hand to stop me, so I take a deep breath.

"Hold on a minute. Let me get this straight," she says. "Aish started a fire and you became water to put it out."

"No," I interrupt her. "I became a wave to save Eden from the strange man. She was near the fire and he was going to grab her. I've been kind of worried about Mordechai, the guy who works with Jacob at the zoo. There's something about him. I can't put my finger on it. I guess he reminds me of the golem."

"How's that?"

"Well, he kind of walks like I remember the golem walking and he always wears a hat. You can never see his forehead. Today, when I made myself into a really powerful wave, the man, whoever he was, got knocked over and his hat fell off. I saw something on his forehead," I say again.

"What did it say?" Miss Sara asks. She sounds both excited and nervous.

I shrug my shoulders. I know I'm letting Miss Sara down. "I was too far away to read it."

"Did anyone else see it?"

"Not that I know of. Ziv didn't. I didn't get to ask anyone

else because Jacob was white-hot with anger about Aish escaping from his cage."

As Miss Sara walks me to the door, she says, "Jordan, you're using your gift to help people in trouble, which is exactly what you're supposed to be doing. You're also keeping your eyes open for the golem. I know it's a big responsibility for you, but I am really thankful that you are doing both of these things."

Miss Sara's words make me happy. I do feel like I'm trying my hardest.

She opens the door. The sun is low behind the elm trees. It's time to be getting home. I shake Miss Sara's hand, step out the door and wave good-bye.

On my way home, I have a tight knot in my stomach. Ima and Abba said somebody might try to kidnap Eden. Was that man trying to take her? Is he the golem? My head spins.

Chapter 15

School Health Week

A FEW days later, toward the end of School Health Week – which is always the second week of school – Ellah and I volunteer to help Nurse Emunah with the first graders.

We line the children up. They're all nervous and jittery. I guess Nurse Emunah's crisp white uniform looks too official. I whistle a little tune from *Sesame Street* and pat the children's heads. That seems to calm them down.

I lead them one at a time to Nurse Emunah, who is sitting at one of the tables wearing her stethoscope. There are swabs, thermometers, and gauze pads in neat piles in front of her. She checks each of the children's noses and then their ears. She listens to their chests with her stethoscope. Then she takes a gauze pad and pushes their tongues down to examine their throats. After the examination, she drops the gauze into a large plastic bag inside a metal trash can at her side.

As the last child steps over to the table to select a prize, either a Chinese kite or a pack of colored felt-tipped pens, Nurse Emunah turns to me. "Jordan, I like the way you've helped me today. Especially the way you kept the kids in line without them being scared."

I nod, embarrassed, and focus my attention on my armband with the red heart.

Ellah, who is just returning from escorting the third grade class back to their room, hears Nurse Emunah's remarks. She smiles at me.

Nurse Emunah pats Ellah on the shoulder. "Ellah, you're great with the kids, too. They really like you."

Ellah smiles. I know she's pleased with the compliment.

Nurse Emunah closes the thick red file with a thump. "We're finished for the day."

"Health Week is such a great idea," Ellah says. "I think all the kids really learned about good health habits this week. Right, Jordan?" Ellah winks at me.

I feel my face flush. I hate it when my face turns red, especially when Ellah is around. "I . . . I think so."

"Chaim," Nurse Emunah calls to the security guard. "Would you please dispose of this bag in the Med-Safety trash container?"

Chaim is the new security guard at our school. He looks up from his table, a baseball cap low over his forehead. A slow smile lights up his face. He marches over to the table, picks up the bag, and drapes it over his shoulder.

"Can we go out for a minute?" Ellah asks Nurse Emunah.

"Sure." Nurse Emunah takes a small blue change purse out of her pocket. She opens it, reaches inside, and hands each of us five shekels. "Go to the makolet and buy yourself a treat." The convenience store is across the street from the school.

"Wow," Ellah and I say simultaneously.

Nurse Emunah just smiles, and then says, "Give me back the armbands. We'll need them again next semester."

We peel off the armbands and hand them back. Then we step outside. We cross the street and head over to Omri's mini-market. Ellah and I both pick a bottle of chocolate milk and pay Omri. Just as we leave the mini-market we see Chaim come out of the school, with the plastic bag over his shoulder. He walks toward his motorcycle.

"I wonder what he's doing," I say. "Isn't the Med-Safety bin on the other side of the school?"

"He looks like he's taking the bag somewhere else. Maybe he's going to throw it in the trash container at the entrance to town. I think they empty it today," Ellah says.

"Nurse Emunah specifically said the Med-Safety container. He's supposed to put it in there. That guy gives me the creeps. He's always staring as though he lost someone and expects to find him at the school." I scratch the top of my head and watch Chaim. "And now he's acting strange."

Chaim turns toward us.

"Watch out! Duck!" I grab Ellah's hand and pull her into the bushes.

Chocolate milk spills down her blouse. Through the leaves I see Chaim stare in our direction. We're crouched down and hidden from view, but still my heart pounds wildly. We watch as Chaim hangs the plastic bag on his motorcycle handles.

"He's going somewhere with that," I whisper.

He looks in our direction again, and then he picks up his helmet and pushes it onto his head without taking his baseball cap off.

"Why does he want those swabs?"

Ellah just shrugs.

Chaim looks up the deserted street one last time. Then he knocks back the kickstand and begins pushing his Yamaha down the street.

"Why is he pushing it, not riding it?" Ellah asks.

"He doesn't want to make noise and attract attention."

"How far is he going to push it?"

I look down the street. "I bet he won't start riding until he gets past the library. Then the noise won't alert anyone."

"I don't get why he wants that bag of mushy gauze, anyways." Ellah snorts.

Suddenly, I remember something my teacher said in science class at the beginning of the week, after a discussion about genes and DNA – the stuff that tells our bodies what to be, carries hereditary traits, and allows for cloning.

"I think he wants the DNA on the gauze," I say.

Ellah shivers. "Jordan, you've got to stop him."

At that moment, I'm a huge wave of water. I collide with the Yamaha, Chaim, and the plastic bag. Chaim falls forward, landing on his overturned bike. Before he gets to his feet, the bag is swept away.

Chaim bangs his fists on the ground in frustration. The bag with the gauze is soaked. After some time he stands, rights his motorcycle, and removes his helmet, careful to keep his baseball cap in place. He slowly drags the Yamaha back to its parking place. Then he strides down the street toward the dripping plastic bag. The cotton gauze pieces are soaked through. He kicks the bag, picks it up, carries it toward the Med-Safety container, and shoves it inside.

Ellah turns toward me. I'm standing right beside her. "Where did you go?" she whispers, annoyed.

"I had to go . . . um . . . to pee," I tell her.

"Out here?" Ellah looks disgusted.

I shrug. I'm sure my face is as scarlet as Ima's strawberries. My cheeks sure are hot.

"You missed the whole thing. A big wave of water knocked Chaim and his motorcycle down. I can't figure out where the water came from. I don't see a broken pipe or anything. Do you?"

I shrug my shoulders.

"The water totally soaked the bag. The swabs must have been ruined. Chaim took the dripping bag and put it into the Med-Safety container," Ellah said. "We're all safe and you missed it."

"Darn," I say. "Let's get back to school."

As we walk down the hall to our next class, we pass the open door of the Attendance Office. I look inside. Miss Sara is standing at the counter reading some papers.

"I'll see you in class," I say to Ellah, and turn into the office.

Miss Sara gasps when I tell her what happened with Chaim and the plastic bag.

"You did the right thing, Jordan. That bag of gauze in the wrong hands could have been a disaster for Kfar Keshet. I'm so proud of you."

I look at my shoes to hide my pleased smile.

"You're really getting good with your gift. I knew you'd be able to control it better and better." As the bell rings, Miss Sara puts an arm over my shoulder and we walk into the empty hall.

"We have two suspects now, Mordechai and Chaim. We have to figure out who Chaim is and why he wanted that bag," Miss Sara says.

"How are you going to find out?" I ask.

"We have our ways," Miss Sara says.

What a mysterious thing to say, I think, but I don't say anything.

Miss Sara grabs me by the shoulders and turns me toward the principal's office. Oh, no, not the principal's office! Before we have a chance to knock, we hear Mr. Portaal's deep voice echoing through the door.

"Don't give me any excuses, Nadav. You should be getting a top grade in science class. You're the son of the principal!"

"But . . ."

I can't hear what Nadav says but I'm kind of smiling to myself. Nadav's not so quick in science either. Mr. Portaal wants Nadav to be perfect. Being the principal's son must be a real downer.

Then Mr. Portaal shouts, "Get to your class now!"

Miss Sara and I step aside as the door swings open and Nadav rushes out, his face red with anger. He glares at me for a second, and then brushes past us and heads toward the stairs to the second floor.

Miss Sara pauses for a moment. Then she raps gently on the door.

"Ca-a-a . . ." Mr. Portaal's voice catches in his throat. There's a loud glumpy sound as he clears his throat. Then he says, "Come in."

Miss Sara pushes the door open and we step inside. Mr. Portaal is wiping his forehead with a white handkerchief. He pushes it back into his jacket pocket and takes a deep breath.

"How can I help you?" he asks briskly, smiling at Miss Sara.

"We've got a problem," she says, as she seats herself in front of his desk.

I'm standing behind Miss Sara's chair. I shift my weight from one foot to the other. Should I sit down?

"Sit down already," Mr. Portaal says to me in an annoyed voice.

I slide into the chair next to Miss Sara. My eyes focus on Mr. Portaal's white socks poking out of his shoes under his desk.

"What's the problem?" Mr. Portaal says.

Miss Sara describes all that Ellah and I just saw outside the school. Mr. Portaal isn't curious about where the wave came from, so Miss Sara doesn't explain it to him.

"What shall we do? Should we fire Chaim?" she asks.

"I don't think so," Mr. Portaal says slowly. "We don't know why he wanted the bag and we don't know if he is acting on his own or working for someone." Mr. Portaal leans back in his chair. "Chaim came very highly recommended. Maybe there's a good explanation for his actions."

I can't think of any explanation for him wanting to take a cruddy bag of gauze, but nobody asks me.

"It's interesting that Mordechai, the guy who works with Jacob at the zoo, is also under suspicion. Jordan thinks that he has something written on his forehead . . . like a golem," Miss Sara says.

"A golem?" Mr. Portaal stares at Miss Sara. "Is there any reason to believe that someone here is a golem?"

Miss Sara nods.

Mr. Portaal exhales heavily. He turns to me, frowning, and asks, "What was on his forehead?"

I shrug my shoulders. "I was too far away to tell."

Mr. Portaal really looks at me, like he's noticing me for the first time. "Why do I keep hearing your name in all of this? Maybe your imagination is just too vivid."

I frown and slump down in the chair. I hate being here. Mr. Portaal doesn't know anything about my imagination or me. Why is Miss Sara putting me through this torture?

"Get back to class," Mr. Portaal commands me with a sweep of his hand. "Sara, we need to speak about this possible danger, if there is any, in private."

I rise from my seat and head for the door. Miss Sara is right behind me. "Don't be discouraged by Mr. Portaal," she whispers to me. "I'm going to insist that he warn the teachers to be careful about any strangers that they see in or around the school." The two o'clock bell rings. I shake Miss Sara's hand and rush up the stairs to class.

Chapter 16

The News Gets Out

LATER that day, Ima meets us after school and we walk into the center of the village.

Ziv looks in the bright windows of the Kfar Keshet coffee shop and smacks his lips. "We haven't had an ice cream treat in a long time," he says.

Mom looks at us and smiles. "You're right. We've all been so busy. Let's have one now."

"Hurrah!" Ziv spins around and claps his hands.

I feel my taste buds tingle. I love ice cream as much as Ziv.

Grinning happily, we follow Ima into the coffee shop. My eyes widen. Nurse Emunah and Chaim are sitting close together at one of the small, round tables. I silently pass their table and look the other way.

"People talk to me all day long, but you're a quiet man," I hear Nurse Emunah say. "I really appreciate your kind of peacefulness."

My face reddens. I can hardly believe my ears.

"Earth to Jordan," Ziv snickers.

I look up. Ziv is waving at me and pointing to a seat at a table close to Chaim and Nurse Emunah.

I quickly pull out the pink and white wire chair and

plunk myself down. I pick up a menu and try to concentrate. Scanning the list of sundaes and milkshakes, I can hear Nurse Emunah's voice. My ears tingle as I focus on their conversation.

"These kids are all so special, but they have the same problems as the other kids at school," I hear Nurse Emunah say. I peek over my menu and see Chaim nodding as though he understands.

"I feel safe talking to you," Nurse Emunah continues. "After all, you are the security guard and you're protecting the children."

I feel like throwing up. Chaim doesn't make me feel safe. The more I look at him, the more I think about the golem.

I hear Ziv order. "I'd like the hot fudge sundae," he says.

I scan the ice cream dishes, but I'm still listening to Nurse Emunah. I tap on the black and white tuxedo sundae, with chocolate and French vanilla, my two favorite ice cream flavors.

The waitress thumps her pencil against her order pad.

"Jordan!" Ima prompts me. "Where's your head? Are you ready to order?"

I hurriedly point at the picture of the black and white tuxedo sundae that I had been tapping.

"That's my favorite," the waitress says as she writes down the order. "I love the chocolate syrup and whipped cream."

I give her one of my "thank you for your cute remark" smiles.

"And then Miss Marks said to the class . . ." Ziv is telling a story I've already heard. As Ziv continues, my ears remain focused on the next table.

I hear Nurse Emunah say, "Of course you've heard about our precious Eden. Just like in the Garden of Eden, our own little animal creator."

I groan inwardly and raise my head. I glance at Nurse

Emunah and Chaim. It seems to me that Chaim is sitting up straighter. Why is she talking about Eden? It's dangerous. Jacob works so hard to keep Eden's amazing gift a secret. Should I interrupt her?

"She has the most extraordinary gift!" Nurse Emunah continues like a windup toy.

The sound of an "aah" escapes from low in Chaim's throat. The vein on his neck is pulsing quickly. He leans forward, staring at Nurse Emunah.

I grab my glass of water and tip my chair. As I fall backwards, I throw the water at Nurse Emunah.

"Oh, no!" she yells as she leaps off her chair. Water is dripping down the front of her uniform.

Ima jumps up, grabs the napkins off the table, and runs over to help Nurse Emunah. I look up. Chaim is standing and staring down at me. I try to look innocent, giving him one of my "I couldn't help it" smiles.

Ziv comes over, untangles me from the chair, and pulls me up. *Another bump on my head,* I think to myself. Ziv gives me a wink and I know he knows that I did it on purpose. Ima is going to kill me.

"Having problems with your chair?" Ima asks as she sits down.

I nod and stare at the floor. I sit down and watch Nurse Emunah and Chaim hurriedly leave the coffee shop.

"Here's your sundae, big boy," the waitress says as she sets the almost overflowing glass bowl on the table in front of me. "Enjoy!"

I stare at the ice cream. I stopped their conversation. Suddenly I'm very hungry.

Chapter 17

The Forgotten Book

T HAT night, after dinner, Ziv and I head upstairs.

"Look how much money I've got," Ziv says. He sweeps his hands through the money in the wooden box in his desk drawer. I hear coins clinking together. "This job is paying great, and I like working with all those strange animals."

"Me too. The cheetah with the ape head is the weirdest."

Ziv nods. "He sure is."

I sigh and lean my elbows on my desk. I stare out the window at the river. "I'm worried," I finally say.

Ziv clinks his coins. "About what? The job is fun!"

"No, not the job itself. But I've got this test in science tomorrow, and because of our job I've hardly had time to study."

"Uh, oh! Your science teacher won't be happy with you if you don't ace that test. Ima and Abba won't be too happy either," Ziv says.

"Duh, I know that." I unzip my backpack and pull out a couple of books.

I lift my backpack and shake it out. Some crumpled papers, a leaky blue pen, and an empty potato chips bag fall to the floor.

I feel my chest tighten. A lump begins forming in my throat. "My science book isn't in here."

"Where is it?" Ziv asks.

"I must have left it at school," I say. Shock makes my voice squeak.

"No way!" Ziv whispers.

There's a long silence.

"I've got to get that book. Ima's going to be so angry. I can't tell her I forgot my book at school again." I scratch my head and tap my fingers on my leg. I start bouncing my foot up and down and turning it in circles nervously. "There has to be a way."

"How? The school's closed. Are you going to go to Mr. Portaal and ask him to open the door? Maybe Nadav has a key." Ziv smirks.

"Shut up. I've got to think." My heart begins to quiver. "I've got a gift. Maybe I can use it."

A small vein twitches on my forehead. Miss Sara's words echo in my ears. *Your gift is a precious thing. You must use it only to help people in trouble. If you do use it for the wrong reasons, you will fail in whatever you're trying to do.*

"I'm in trouble, right?" I say, looking Ziv in the eye.

"Well, I don't know if you are now, but you sure will be tomorrow."

"Miss Sara told me to only use my gift for people in trouble, and I'm in trouble, so I think I can use my gift."

"It all depends on what she means by trouble," Ziv says.

"What do you mean?"

"Well, if she means saving a person from a mountain lion, or from drowning, or from falling into a ditch, that's one kind of trouble," Ziv reasons.

"What if I don't get my book and I fail the test?" My heart is thumping. "And Abba doesn't let me go near the river and someone drowns because I'm not there? Wouldn't that seem like asking for trouble?"

"Did she say 'asking for trouble,' or 'trouble'?" Ziv asks.

"She said 'trouble,' but I've got a working definition for trouble which lets me use my gift."

"Whatever." Ziv shrugs.

I have to do something. I need to pass the test or I'll flunk science class and have to take it again.

"I have to find my book!"

"Jordan, you're in big trouble," Ziv says. "Last time you forgot your book Ima said, 'Tsk, tsk, second time this semester, Jordan.'" Ziv mimics Ima's high voice.

I laugh for a second at Ziv's imitation. Then my smile droops. "Aw, shut up, Ziv! You sound just like Nadav."

"I do not, you creep," growls Ziv. "I'm not anything like Nadav. He's all mean and tricky." Ziv's voice quivers.

"Okay, you aren't like him."

"And Nadav stole Noam's tadpoles."

"I know. He does sneaky things. I don't trust him. School was much more fun before Mr. Portaal and Nadav came back."

Ziv nods and opens his math book.

"I knew right away. Nadav's trouble. It's those black eyes – like an alien."

"Right," Ziv says as he pulls his lids back and rolls his eyes.

"I've got an idea." I can feel my face warm up.

"Yeah?"

"If Noam can make a cloud cover that full moon, I can go into the school and get my book."

"Why cover the moon?"

"I don't want anyone to know I'm using my gift to go into the school. The fewer people who know, the better."

Ziv nods and closes his math book.

It's decided. We race downstairs.

"We're on our way to Noam's house," I yell to Ima, who's upstairs.

"It's a school night," she calls down.

"Yeah, we know. We won't be gone long."

"Abba's at the village council meeting. He'll be home about ten. Watch the time and get home early."

"No problem," I call.

It's a warm, late September night. The frogs are croaking at the full moon. The cloudless night sky is littered with stars.

"Let's take that shortcut across Mr. Goldman's field," I say.

"Do we have to?" Ziv asks. He wrinkles his nose. "It's so scary!"

"It's the quickest way to Noam's house. We need to get there fast!"

"I don't know, Jordan . . ."

"Give me your hand. I'm not scared."

In the field there's amber colored wheat, now gray in the moonlight. I hold Ziv's hand as we begin to walk quickly along the shortcut.

"I hope no one sees us," Ziv says. "It's embarrassing, you holding my hand."

As the path narrows, I follow behind Ziv. He looks up for a second and stumbles over something.

He lurches and falls forward. "Ow! My toe!"

I bend to pick him up.

He brushes the dirt off his knees. "I hate this wheat field!"

In the light of the full moon, I can see tears are running down his red, flushed face. There are all kinds of things living here. Crawly creatures . . . like snakes and rats and things.

He kicks at the sheaves near the path. "It gives me the creeps!" Ziv says.

"Don't worry! Come on!" I grab his trembling hand. "We're almost at Noam's house."

We keep hurrying through the grasses. As we get to the end of the field, Ziv slips again, lurches forward, and pulls me over.

"Hey, watch where you're going," I yell.

He gets up and brushes himself off.

"You look like a wheat sheaf, Ziv," I pull wheat kernels out of his shirt and hair.

"You do, too."

We stand up and brush off the remaining wheat in our hair and clothes. Then we cross the road. We find Noam in his garden, looking up at the sky through his telescope.

"Does he ever stop playing with that?" I whisper.

Ziv shrugs.

"Hey, Noam, what's up?"

Noam swivels around and smiles. "Well, Venus is—"

"Forget it. I didn't come for an astronomy lesson. I need your help."

"My help?" Noam steps back from the telescope. "What's happening?"

I kick at a tuft of grass at my feet. "I need to get into the school. I forgot my science book."

"Geez. That's a bad one. How are you going to get in?"

"Well, I thought I would experiment with my gift."

"Didn't you get the 'you only use this gift to help people in trouble' speech?"

"Sure I did. *I'll* be in trouble if I don't get that book."

"What's your gift?" Noam asks.

"It's a secret. Will you take the secrecy oath?"

"Sure," Noam answers quickly.

We stand in a circle.

"Repeat after me," I say seriously. *"Aleph, aleph, beit, beit*, swear to heaven and never forget."

Noam repeats the oath. Then we all do the secret handshake.

"I guess we're like double-brothers now. Second time

we've done the oath this year!" Noam says in an excited whisper. Ziv and I nod.

"I've always wanted a brother. You guys don't know what it's like. Three sisters. It just about drives me crazy."

Three sisters don't sound so bad to me. I've only got Ziv. Noam's talk about his sisters makes me think about Ellah for a second. Thinking about her always gives me a warm feeling in my chest.

"You're not going to believe this." I take a moment to look around the yard. "I can flow like water under locked doors."

"Hey, that's really neat!" Noam says in an excited voice.

"And you? I know you do things with clouds," I say.

"I can feel like a cloud."

"Do you fly up to the sky?"

"No. Not really. When I begin to feel like a cloud, I usually end up in some tall tree or on someone's roof."

"Wow!" I say.

"Shh," Ziv says suddenly and puts a finger to his lips. He points to a tree that shades the backyard. "Someone's over there."

We run over to the tree. Ellah is sitting there holding a flashlight. "What's all of the 'aleph, aleph, beit, beit' stuff for this time?"

"Nothing for you to know, Sis," Noam says crossly. "What are you doing here?"

"This yard isn't yours, you know. Just because your telescope's here doesn't mean you own it." Ellah sticks out her tongue at Noam.

"Sisters!" Noam says, exasperated.

"What are you guys doing anyways?" Ellah persists. "Are you going to the school or something?"

"The school is closed, you know," I manage to say, even though my heart has skipped a beat.

"Well then, where are you going?"

"It's none of your business, snoopy," Noam snaps. "This is a guy thing."

"Don't yell at me, starry head."

Noam lunges toward Ellah. She takes a quick step to the side.

"Too late! Ha, ha!" She sticks out her tongue.

"I'll get you, you little—" Noam stops short as the back door screeches open.

We all look up.

"Ell-llah, are you bothering Noam again?"

Their mother steps outside. "Come in, young lady. Right now!"

Noam snickers as Ellah rushes toward the house. The back door slams shut.

"Phew, that was close!" I say. "I never thought we'd get rid of her. I need you to help cover the moon with the clouds and I need Ziv to grab the book. Ellah can't do anything to help us tonight. I'm glad your mom called her." I wipe the sweat off my forehead. "What's she doing out here anyway?"

"You know Ellah," Noam whispers. "She loves crawly things – especially spiders. She comes out at night to watch them."

"I hate them," Ziv whispers back.

"Does she still collect them?" I ask, curious. "I thought that was a summer thing."

"She doesn't really collect them. She just watches them," Noam says.

"Ugh," Ziv says, wrinkling up his nose.

"She's watched them for so long, she's learned to weave her own spider webs."

"Wow! That's kinda neat," Ziv admits. "What does she do with them?"

"She hangs some of them in her room and she gives some away. You remember my basketball bag?"

Ziv nods.

"That's one of the webs she copied."

"You're kidding!"

"By the way, Ziv, how did you see her in the garden?" Noam stares at Ziv. "I didn't see anyone."

"It's my gift," Ziv says, grinning, "I see people's colors."

"People have colors?" Noam asks, surprised.

Ziv nods.

"Geez, that's amazing."

"Listen, it's getting late and I need my book. Noam, are you still with us?" I ask.

"Of course!"

"Do you have to tell your parents you're going?" Ziv asks.

"No. I usually stay out till real late. Ima and Abba are always asleep when I go inside," Noam says.

"Let's go then! I'll tell you what you need to do on the way," I say.

We walk out the front gate like the three musketeers and turn on to Jabotinsky Road. The night sky is bright from the full moon and all the glittering stars.

Noam looks back at his house for a minute. "I hope Ellah isn't peeking out of her window," he says. "She can be a real pain sometimes."

Ziv nods his head.

"What would you know about it?" I challenge. "You haven't got a sister."

Ziv shrugs his shoulders.

"We should walk in the shadows so no one sees us," Noam says.

"Good idea," I say.

We walk along the road to the school, staying close to the tall trees that grow along the sidewalk. The full moon illuminates the road so well that it's nearly as light as daytime. We turn on to Beit Sefer Drive.

"There are a lot of people out tonight," Ziv whispers.

"There's Ro'i walking Smokey."

A long-haired teenage boy is reading a book and walking slowly with a large Dalmatian. The dog turns to look at us a couple of times, but Ro'i doesn't seem to notice. At the corner he turns up Herzl Street, still unaware that we've been walking behind him.

"Look!" Noam points across the street. "That's whatshisname's father."

"Rephael's father," Ziv says, "and his name is Shlomo."

"Watch out," I whisper as I jump to the side. Shlomo jogs past without glancing at us.

Next, a young couple I don't know but I've seen around walk slowly up the street toward us and almost bump into us.

"What luck! They didn't even see us." I twirl my finger near my ear and make the cuckoo sign. "They were just staring at each other."

Ziv and Noam giggle.

"There's the school," I say. We all stop under the towering elm trees beside the closed market, across the street from the school. The school building looks unwelcoming. The leaves of the trees blowing in the breeze are making jagged shadow pictures on the walls.

"Why does it look so spooky?" Ziv asks quietly.

"It's not scary during the day. Are you sure you want to go in there?"

"No problem," I answer at once, even though my heart is beating like a bongo drum. "I know it looks dark. All I need to do is flow in, get my book, unlock the door, give it to you, lock the door, and come back out. It'll be a piece of cake."

"Good luck," Noam says, shaking his head.

"Noam, I need you to hide the light of the moon. Can you do that?" I ask.

Noam nods. "It'll take a couple of minutes. I don't have any clouds to work with. Let me get started."

We sit down on the curb and look up at the sky. Above the school we see a small cloud forming. "Hey Noam, that's great," I say, turning to my friend, but he's vanished. I look around quickly but I still don't see him. "Where'd he go?"

"Psst. I'm up here."

Ziv and I look up. Noam is sitting in the elm tree, way up at the top.

"Be careful," I gulp. I've fallen out of enough trees to know how dangerous it is.

"Don't worry, I'm fine," Noam says quietly. He turns his head toward the growing cloud mass.

"Look, the cloud's getting bigger and bigger."

Ziv points at the sky.

I'm beginning to feel antsy. I hope this doesn't take much longer.

"Psst!" We look up to the top of the tree. "Go now," Noam orders. "I can't hold it here forever."

There is a cloud covering the moon. I shiver.

Chapter 18

The Break-In

ZIV and I jump up. In almost complete darkness we rush across the street, jog up the five wide steps to the school and stop in front of the thick wooden door. I flash a thumbs-up sign to Noam. He's still up in the tree. I hope he can see us in the now-moonless night.

"You just wait out here," I say to Ziv. "I'll go in and get the book. I'll open the door and hand it to you." I wait for Ziv to nod.

"Can't I go with you?"

"How're you going to go with me, stupid? You can't flow under the door."

"I don't want to be standing here for a long time. Someone's going to see me."

"You're scared."

"Am not."

"You are."

"I just don't want anyone to see me."

"Okay, fine. I'll open the door and you can come inside while I get the book."

As quickly as I can, I get my water words to fill my head and I flow under the door and into the school. I re-form as fast as I can and quickly unlock the door and pull Ziv inside. Then I shut the door and lock it. We walk over to the row of lockers along the wall.

"Look, here's my book in my locker just where I left it," I say, as I close my locker door.

Ziv nods and then whispers a request in my ear.

"You always have to go to the bathroom," I snarl. "Can't you wait?"

"No, I need to go now."

My eyes are quickly adjusting to the dark. "I can see. Can you?"

Ziv nods.

"Follow me." I head for the wide stairs. The bathrooms are upstairs. On the fourth step, the annoying science book slips out of my hands and tumbles down the stairs. It lies spread-eagled on the ground floor.

"Don't leave me," Ziv says.

I look at Ziv and then at my book. "All right. I'll pick it up on the way down."

"It's so quiet here. It makes me nervous," Ziv says.

"Okay. I'll hold the door open and wait out here, but hurry."

I stand at the open bathroom door, whistling a tune so Ziv knows I'm here.

Suddenly a long roll of thunder echoes through the school. Ziv runs out of the bathroom tugging on his zipper. "That was scary!" he whispers as the thunder peal rolls away.

"What was that?" We hear a distant voice from the first floor.

Ziv and I stare at each other, our eyes huge.

"Someone's in the building," Ziv whispers into my ear.

"Shh!" I say.

"What's this?" the voice asks, "a puddle of water and a science book." A pause. "It's Jordan's science book."

I'd recognize that nasty voice anywhere. "It's Nadav," I

whisper as we strain to listen. "He's talking to someone. Who else is in the school?"

"Jordan thinks he's so smart. He didn't even take his book home before the test," Nadav's voice reaches us. "Such a snot. Thinks he owns the river. I hope he fails the stupid test. Come on, Nitzan. We have work to do."

I clench my fists. My breath is coming hard. Then we hear the book thrown to the floor. I jerk toward the stairs. "I'll kill him!"

"Jordan!" Ziv hisses fiercely. He grabs my arm and pulls me back from the stairs.

What? I want to say, but don't.

"Let's go home!"

I shake my head. "We've got to find out why they're here."

"No, we don't! We can just sneak out."

"Don't be a baby! Wait here."

"Don't leave me."

"Okay. Come on! But be quiet."

We shake off our sandals and place them behind the bathroom door.

Like two shadows we sneak down the stairs and tiptoe through the hall. Without a sound, we press ourselves into a corner of the tall bookcase opposite the Attendance Office. In the dark office, Nadav and Nitzan are noisily opening desk drawers and file cabinets.

"It has to be here somewhere," Nadav says. "If we don't find that test I'm going to fail science class!"

That's it. Nadav is trying to steal the test. I drop to my knees and start to crawl toward the door.

"Did you know I can see in the dark?" Nadav says. "I always thought everyone could," he says with a snort. "Then I found out it was something special."

I scramble back from the door and crawl furiously to Ziv. "His gift is to see in the dark," I whisper. "We've got to get away from here. He'll see us. Come on!"

We race toward the staircase, past my textbook, as Nadav and Nitzan continue to rifle through the office drawers. I take Ziv's shaking hand and we slowly tiptoe up the stairs to wait for them to leave. I can't go home without my book.

The third step creaks.

"What was that?" Nitzan's voice shakes. "I heard something."

From halfway up the stairs, I see Nadav look up and down the hall.

Ziv and I stand frozen. We're hardly breathing.

"Don't worry about it," Nadav says. "It's just this old creaky building. Let's find the test paper and get out of this stinking place. I've always hated this school and the nerdy kids who go here."

I hear him walk back into the office. After a moment he shouts, "Here it is. I've found it. Now all I have to do is make a copy and I'm home free. Hurray!"

"One copy? What about me?" Nitzan says.

"Of course," Nadav says. "I meant one for you and one for me."

There is a rustle of paper and the buzz of the copier.

"Wouldn't my father be surprised if he found out you and I were in the school?" Nadav says.

I hear a smile in his voice. I imagine he's grinning.

Ziv and I raise our eyebrows at each other.

"Look out the window," we hear Nadav order Nitzan. "Is anyone out there?" A pause. "No? Okay, let's go."

We hear the scrambling sound of shoes. The front door squeaks open and closes. Click, click, and then there is silence. My heart is racing, but I still can't move.

"They stole the science test!" My voice rises into a squeak. "They just walked in and stole the test."

Ziv nods. His eyes are wide.

"Let's get out of here," I say.

We pull on our sandals and creep down the stairs. At the bottom, I dart over to the window near the front door and look out.

"It's all clear, Ziv," I whisper. I'm still whispering, even though we're alone in the school.

We scurry into the Attendance Office.

"Would ya look at this?" I give a low whistle. "Not a paper out anywhere."

"I was sure they'd leave a mess," Ziv groans. "Now no one will ever know they stole the test."

"We've gotta get out of here." I yank Ziv's hand. We leave the Attendance Office and race toward the door.

"Where's your book?" Ziv asks.

"Oh, gosh! I almost forgot." I laugh nervously as I bend over and pick up the book.

"Here, you take it." I hand the science book to Ziv.

Then we both peek out the window. The street seems empty. I unlock the lock and pull on the door handle, but the door doesn't budge. "The door is stuck."

"Stuck?"

I try it again. I relock and unlock the door again. I give a mighty pull but the big wooden door refuses to open.

"Oh, no! They've double locked the door," I say.

"So?"

Ziv doesn't understand.

"So, we can't unlock it."

"You opened it before," Ziv says.

"Yes, but only the lower lock was locked. The security guard must have forgotten to lock the upper one. Now that's locked, too. We haven't got the key."

"So now what?" Ziv asks, staring around wildly.

"I don't know. There's gotta be a way to get you out of here."

There's a sudden scratching at the window. We both jump.

I peer cautiously out the window. Noam is standing there, a couple of leaves stuck in his hair. Through the security bars, I push hard on the window and it scrapes open.

"Are you two okay?" Noam's voice is all strained and shaky. He looks up and down the street. "I saw Nadav and Nitzan go in and out. I made the lightning and the thunderclap to warn you. What were they after?"

I shrug my shoulders. "The science test."

Noam rolls his eyes. "You're kidding. Did they see you guys?"

I shake my head.

"Come on. Let's go. My cloud is going to break up soon."

I find my voice. "You go on. We've got a problem."

I explain the issue to Noam.

"Oy, that's bad." He shakes his head. "What are you gonna do?"

"I'm not sure yet. I'll think of something. You go home."

"Are you sure?"

"Yeah, we'll be fine. Hey, your cloud was great."

"Thanks." Noam smiles. "You're sure you're okay? I could stay a little longer."

"Naw, we'll be fine. See you tomorrow."

We wave at each other. "Go home, Noam. I don't want your parents looking for you. See you tomorrow."

I force the window shut.

"Well, now what?" Ziv asks, his eyes enormous.

I sit down on the bottom step of the stairs inside the school. "We have to get you out somehow," I mutter, half to myself. I shake my head to clear out the cobwebs that are making it hard to think.

"How?" Ziv whispers.

I shrug my shoulders. Ziv's eyes fill with tears.

"Hold on, Ziv!" I say brusquely. "If we don't find another way, we'll sleep in the school until tomorrow. Won't the secretary be surprised when she opens the door and two students are already in the school?"

I make a face and Ziv begins to laugh.

"That would really be funny," Ziv says. "We'd be the first pupils at the school . . . like we were so anxious to get to school that we slept on the floor."

Ziv stops laughing.

I'm not laughing anymore either. "Ziv, I need to go for help."

"Where will you go?"

"I don't know yet. I'll think of something. I'll flow out of the school and see where I end up. The best person would be Miss Sara." I hope she won't be too angry with me.

Ziv nods.

"You'll have to stay here by yourself. You'll have to be brave."

"I'm not so sure . . ."

"You walked through Mr. Goldman's field. That was brave."

"But you were with me."

"Listen, Ziv," I say as calmly as I can. "Ima and Abba are probably really worried. It's late. I haven't even studied for the test yet. I'm responsible for getting you out of here and I can't do anything from inside."

"You know how I hate to be in dark places by myself."

"This is the school. You know this place. The cloud will

be breaking up really fast and you'll have a lot of moonlight to see by."

Ziv begins to sniff.

"You can even go and lie down on Mr. Portaal's brown couch. What do you think of that?"

"I don't have his permission."

"I give you permission. It will be our secret."

Ziv nods, his lips pressed together.

Ziv's already eleven. Why is he acting like such a baby? "Either I go out or we sleep here tonight. Which do you want?"

Fat tears roll down Ziv's cheeks. "I'll stay here and wait for you," he says.

"Okay, then," I say. "Don't worry. It'll be all right." I brought us into this mess. I have to get us out of it.

I push open the door to Mr. Portaal's office. Inside is a brown leather sofa with a plaid blanket at one end. It stands against the back wall, between two filing cabinets. Ziv takes a deep breath and moves slowly toward the sofa.

"Ziv, you'll be fine on Mr. Portaal's sofa," I say. "Should I shut the door or leave it open?"

Ziv snuggles into the plaid afghan and looks at me through fearful eyes. "I . . . I don't know." His voice trembles.

"I'll close it," I say gently. "Just like at home. Okay?"

Ziv shrugs under the afghan.

"I'm going for help now. Just stay here. Don't be scared, I'll be back soon. You'll be out in no time." I bend over and for the first time in a long time kiss Ziv on the forehead.

Ziv smiles at me. "Just hurry," he says. "All I want to do is go home and sleep in my own bed."

"I know. Me, too," I say, and gently close the door.

Chapter 19

Going for Help

I RACE quickly to the front door. My heart is drumming wildly. I remember Miss Sara's warning the day I got my gift. *Only use your gift to help people who are in trouble,* she said. Forgetting my book wasn't the kind of trouble she was talking about. I'm pretty sure of that now. But now I don't have a choice. I have to save Ziv – he is in trouble.

I take a deep breath and try to concentrate. I think of my water words. I say them over and over. After a moment I feel the smooth sensation of water going around and through me, then a slight pinch as I flow under the locked door. I'm flowing past grass and little bits of twigs. I'm traveling uphill. I thicken over a brick pathway, then I flatten out as I'm pushed under a narrow opening. Suddenly I'm in the house. My arms and legs start to form. I look around. I stand up. I hear a slight cough.

Miss Sara is sitting in her rocking chair staring at me.

I'm so relieved I do a little dance.

"Hello, Jordan," Miss Sara says quietly. "You're out late tonight, aren't you?"

"I need help!" I groan as I continue to re-form as quickly as I can. I'm trembling and my words pour out like an overturned soda bottle. "Ziv is in the school. The door is double locked. He's waiting for me on Mr. Portaal's couch without Mr. Portaal's permission. I can't get him out to take him home and I'm going to fail my science test."

Miss Sara rises from her rocking chair and hurries toward me. She puts an arm around my shoulder. "Jordan, Jordan, calm down. One thing at a time."

I'm out of breath and shaking all over. I inhale deeply and in a hoarse voice I explain as best as I can how Ziv got locked in the school. But I don't say anything about Nadav and Nitzan.

"I didn't mean to do anything wrong," I whimper. "I just thought I could use my gift to get into the school and grab my book. I didn't mean to cause any trouble."

Miss Sara nods and looks gravely at me. "We'll talk about that later. Now we need to rescue Ziv. He must be so nervous." Miss Sara pauses and looks at her bookshelf, then back at me. "There's just one thing I don't understand. If you could get into the school and open the door and let Ziv in, why couldn't you open the door to let him out?"

"I told you," I say in an exasperated voice. "The school door was double locked. I couldn't open it."

"So when you went into the school, only one lock was locked?"

I nod.

"But when you wanted Ziv to leave with your book, the top lock was locked."

I nod again.

"How did it get double locked?" Miss Sara asks.

I shrug my shoulders and look down. The only sound is my right shoe scraping back and forth on the floor.

"Something strange happened at the school tonight," Miss Sara says.

I don't look up.

"No matter," she says at last. "We must get Ziv out of the

school immediately. I'm not sure if my keys still work, but we can try."

Miss Sara leaves the room. I hear her rummaging through a drawer in the kitchen.

"Well here they—" she begins to say when she is interrupted by a knock at her front door. "This is turning into a busy night," she remarks as she rushes to the door and swings it open.

I peek out from behind Miss Sara's back where I am hiding.

"Jordan! What are you doing here?"

Through the open door, I see Ima and Abba.

"I . . . I . . ." I stutter.

"We need your help to rescue Ziv," Miss Sara says to my parents, saving me from answering.

"Ziv! What's wrong with Ziv?" Abba looks from me to Miss Sara.

"He's locked in the school and we have to get him out," Miss Sara says with authority.

"He's locked in the school?" Abba sounds more puzzled than angry.

"My poor baby," Ima groans.

"How did this happen?" Abba glares at me.

I look at the floor and sniff loudly. I feel something wet around my eyes.

"We don't have time to talk about it now!" Miss Sara says quickly. "Just follow me!"

We all hurry out of the house.

"Let me have the keys. I can walk faster than you," Abba says to me. I look at my hand. I'm still holding the keys Miss Sara gave me at the front door. I toss him the keys and we walk side by side.

"When I unlock the door, where will I find Ziv?" Abba asks.

"I left him in Mr. Portaal's office, lying on his sofa."

The sky is now completely clear of clouds and it's easy to follow the path to Menachem Begin Road. Abba arrives at the school first. He bends over, panting and sweating, and wipes his forehead with his sleeve. Then he pulls the keys out of his front pocket, selects one, and slips it into the lock. The key turns. Then he chooses another key and tries to fit it into the dead bolt, but it won't go. He looks carefully at all of the keys on the ring.

I catch up with him. I'm sweating and panting and it takes a moment before I can speak.

"What are you waiting for?" I finally ask.

"I don't have a key for the upper lock," Abba says as he tries the rest of the keys. "None of these seem to fit."

My face turns white. "What are we going to do?"

The two of us look up. Miss Sara and Ima are almost at the school.

"How did Ziv get into the school in the first place?" Abba asks.

I study my shoes.

"Well?"

"Well, I was using my gift," I start to explain.

"Wait a minute," I hear Ima say, "I want to hear this, too." She stands next to us, breathing heavily.

"Gee, Ima," I begin nervously. "I wanted to tell you . . . but . . . it was kind of late and you were asleep and . . . I didn't have my book . . . and . . ."

Ima and Abba stare at me. They know I'm forbidden to use my gift to do things like picking up a book I forgot at school. Miss Sara is frowning. She warned me. Use your gift incorrectly and everything will go wrong, she said. Boy, was she right.

Miss Sara coughs into her hand. "It seems as though he forgot the warning I gave him when he became aware of his gift."

I gulp. My cheeks heat up.

"Because of his childishness he has used his gift incorrectly. He has acted wrongly and I am very unhappy and upset with him," Miss Sara continues.

Tears are trickling down my cheeks, but I wipe them away as quickly as I can.

"None of your keys fit this upper lock," Abba says. "What should we do?"

"I guess we'll have to go to the principal's house and see if he has a new key," Miss Sara says.

"Mr. Portaal's house?" I gasp.

Miss Sara nods her head. "I'm afraid so. But you're not coming with us. I don't think Ziv wants to stay in the school alone. He needs you to keep him company."

The light-headed relief I feel when I learn I don't have to go to Mr. Portaal's house is wiped away when Miss Sara says I have to go back into the school to be with Ziv.

She is looking at me with her serious face. "Go to Ziv. Tell him that we're getting the key and we'll be back with it as soon as we can."

"But what if Mr. Portaal is angry or—"

"Jordan, do as I tell you, right now," Miss Sara cuts me off. "You'll have to worry about Mr. Portaal later."

I walk over to the curb and sit down. My eyes are heavy with tears. My face is flushed, my heart is racing. Miss Sara has never spoken to me like this before. I'm so upset that I find I can't activate my gift.

Abba walks over to me. "Well, go ahead now Jordan!"

I shake my head. I just can't do it.

Ima comes over. She sits down at the curb and put her arms around me. "It will be okay," she comforts me. "You've made a big mistake and you'll have to face that, but right now you must go back to Ziv. I know you can. Stop crying and do whatever it is you do." She pats me on the shoulder. "Go ahead." Ima kisses me on the forehead. "You can do it. Ziv is waiting for you."

I dry my eyes and take several ragged breaths. I begin to think of the words that make me into water. Flow, row, ripple, tumble, smooth . . . I say them over and over until the familiar feeling of water washes over me. I feel little nubs of grass bending under my weight as I flatten out. I wash up the school's front steps and sweep under the locked door.

I open my eyes. I've re-formed. I'm on the stairs inside the school and it's very quiet. I look down. My book is still on the floor where I left it. I ignore it. I need to go to Ziv. I tiptoe toward Mr. Portaal's office, silently open the door and look inside. Asleep on Mr. Portaal's sofa, Ziv is breath-

ing noisily. The plaid blanket lies crumpled on the floor.

I don't wake him. If I tell him Mr. Portaal may be coming he'll get sniffly and weepy. I'll just wait for the waterworks, I guess. I sit down in Mr. Portaal's big comfortable leather chair. I begin to feel more relaxed, and my eyes start to droop. I need to stay awake.

I shake myself, get up, and walk around the office. I go out to the hallways and then to the school's front door. I look outside. The street is deserted. It's sure taking them a long time. I pick up my book and walk back to Mr. Portaal's office.

I sit down again in Mr. Portaal's chair and open my book. It's really hard to study in this room. I absentmindedly twirl around in the chair, then I pick up one of the pens lying on the blotter and tap out a tune on the desk. Ziv turns over and mumbles something in his sleep. I stop tapping and put the pen down. Quietly, I open and close a couple of drawers on the principal's desk. I inspect his paperclips and staplers. Then I just sit, staring at my open book. After a while, I cross my arms and lay my head down on Mr. Portaal's desk.

Chapter 20

Mr. Portaal Appears

'M floating lazily. Cool, clear water streams through my wavy hair. I swim and float in the lake. A small silver fish darts past. I grab for it. Darn, missed again. I sink, then rise, and start blowing air bubbles.

Scrape!

I jerk upright. The lake disappears.

Another scrape! Awake now, I hear the school door slam shut.

"I still don't understand how Jordan and Ziv broke in." Mr. Portaal's voice echoes loudly in the hall.

I flinch.

"They didn't exactly break in," I hear Abba say.

"Look over here," Mr. Portaal grumbles. "Do you see that puddle of water? I hope they haven't done any other damage."

"It's just a small spot of water," Abba says. "I wouldn't call it 'damage.' "

The footsteps draw closer.

"I guess we have different takes on this affair," Mr. Portaal says after a moment. "I suppose if my son were involved I would feel protective, too. Where do you think the boys are?"

"Jordan told me Ziv was in your office."

"In my office? Why would they go into my office? No one goes in there unless I invite them."

"I guess we'll have to ask them," Abba says calmly.

I look around wildly. Ziv is still sound asleep on the sofa. I've got to get Mr. Portaal's plaid blanket off the floor where it's lying in a heap after Ziv turned over. I lurch toward the couch. The door swings opens. Mr. Portaal stares at me.

"Well I'll be," the principal says. "Would you look at him, standing next to my desk? And over there, on my sofa . . ." His eyes behind his glasses are huge saucers.

Abba peers into the room. Ima isn't with him.

I run to my father and grab hold of his hand. "Oh, Abba, am I happy to see you. Where's Ima?"

"She's walking Miss Sara home," he whispers. "I think the shock of this was too much for her."

"I'm not happy to see you," Mr. Portaal says acidly. "What are you and Ziv doing in my office in the middle of the night?"

"Well . . ." I begin, my voice shaking. "I . . . I forgot my science book in school."

"And . . . ?" Mr. Portaal encourages me. "You forgot your science book at school, and . . . ?"

"Well, I didn't know what to do, so I thought—"

Before I can continue, Mr. Portaal says, "So you decided to break into the school to get your book."

"Well, no, not exactly. I didn't break in . . . I—"

"What do you call this? Just because you went under the door like water instead of through it doesn't mean it wasn't a break-in."

I shrug.

"Do you have any idea what would happen to our school if every student decided to break in when he forgot something?"

"No, sir," is the only answer I can think of. Shaking my

head, I look at my hands. Mr. Portaal leans against his desk. "You do know that we can't allow this to happen, right?"

"Right!" I whisper through dry lips.

"Not ever . . ."

"Shhhh," Ziv says groggily. "Can't you see I'm trying to sleep?"

Everyone looks at Ziv stretched out on the sofa. Abba walks over and sits down next to him. "Ziv," he calls. "Ziv." He gently pats Ziv's head.

Ziv opens his sleepy eyes and looks around. Mr. Portaal is glaring at him. Ziv gasps and scrambles to his feet.

"I'm sorry I'm on your sofa, Mr. Portaal," he blurts out.

Mr. Portaal is as silent as a stone. A mean look stretches across his face.

"I was so scared and sleepy and Jordan had to leave me alone in the school because of the top lock. He said I could stay in your office because I was scared. He closed the door like at home."

Ziv stops to catch his breath and then rushes on. "I was tired. And your sofa looked like it was waiting for me to lie down on it. Do you know what I mean?" Ziv stops again and looks around the room a minute. He gulps and then hurriedly reaches down and slips his sandals on.

Mr. Portaal folds his arms across his chest. "Ziv, I know that something strange happened at the school tonight. I don't exactly understand what. Do you want to explain it to me?"

"Well," Ziv begins, "Jordan forgot his science book."

"Yes, we've established that fact," Mr. Portaal says.

"And he couldn't take the book out when he was water, so I said I would help him . . . and then I had to pee so we went into the school . . ."

"Yes . . ."

"And then we heard this noise . . ." Ziv looks at me.

Everyone is looking at him. I quickly shake my head. He pauses for a second. He coughs. He looks at me again. "Then we were locked in. That's what happened." Ziv drops back onto the sofa and jiggles his legs nervously.

"Why is it that I never seem to get to the end of this story?" Mr. Portaal looks from me to Ziv. "For some reason, neither of you is prepared to tell me what I would like to know. How did you enter the school without a problem and then get locked inside?"

Ziv looks at the floor.

"It just happened," I say after a long silence and shrug. I'm not going to tell Mr. Portaal about Nadav. He won't believe me and I can't prove it.

While we are standing looking at each other, at an impasse, we hear the heavy wooden door to the school screeching open again.

"Hello, hello?" I recognize the voice. It's Mr. Freed, the sergeant. "Who's there?" he asks in a loud voice.

"In here," Mr. Portaal shouts. "Everything's okay."

Footsteps echo in the empty hall. In a minute, Mr. Freed, in his blue uniform, steps into the principal's office.

"Hi, Shimon," he says to the principal. The two men shake hands.

The sergeant turns to us. "Kinda late for school, isn't it?" He smiles.

Ziv and I study the floor.

"I saw lights on when I walked past," Mr. Freed explains. "I thought I would step inside and see what's happening."

"Well, we've had a situation," Mr. Portaal says, "but I think everything is under control now."

"Does this have anything to do with the two guys Ro'i saw leaving the school a couple of hours ago?"

"What?" we all say together.

"Ro'i was out walking Smokey. He saw some kids rushing out of the school. He wasn't wearing his glasses . . . typical

MR. FREED

מר פריד

of him, so he can't identify them." Mr. Freed chuckles. "He never wears his glasses if he can avoid it. He thinks Smokey is a Seeing Eye dog or something." Mr. Freed laughs again, apparently not noticing the tension in the room.

"Who were the two kids?" Mr. Portaal says, as if to himself.

"I don't know. He couldn't tell," Mr. Freed says.

"This story gets murkier and murkier." Mr. Portaal shakes his head. "Is there a chance that you two know who Ro'i saw while he was out walking?"

Ziv looks quickly at me. We both shake our heads.

The principal clasps his hands behind his back and paces up and down.

"Listen, Shimon," Abba says. "It's ten-thirty. Jordan has a test tomorrow, with or without his book. He needs to go to sleep."

Mr. Portaal nods slowly. "I guess we'll have to sort this out in the morning."

I bend over to pick up the plaid blanket and fold it.

"Just leave it, Jordan!" Mr. Portaal snaps. "It's late now and I'm letting you out but that doesn't mean I've forgotten all the trouble you two boys have caused. Go home!"

I drop the blanket on the sofa.

"Deb and I will try to get to the bottom of this," Abba says as he takes both of us by the hand. He looks sternly at us. "You can be sure they will be punished."

"I would be very strict about this. Children shouldn't feel they can break into school whenever they want."

"We will make that very clear to them." Abba says sharply. "Come on, boys. Let's go home."

I quickly slip past Mr. Portaal and grab my book off his desk. Then we all leave the office.

Abba, Ziv, and I walk out the front door, down the steps, and turn homeward. As we walk home, Abba holds our wrists like we're handcuffed. The full moon is shining on the deserted streets. A dog barks. In the surrounding fields of the village, goats and sheep bleat. I listen to the sound of the water flowing from the river, just gurgling along. I wish I could jump into the river right now. I would sink all the way to the bottom and just lie there for a while.

Ziv walks along. I watch him looking up at Abba. He tries to slow his pace, but Abba keeps pulling him along. This is going to be a bad night.

As the three of us enter the tunnel of trees near our house, I take a deep breath. The house lights are on. Ima is sitting outside on the front porch. She stands up as she sees us, and when we finally reach her, she hugs and kisses Ziv and me.

"I've been waiting a long time," she says tiredly. "I walked Miss Sara home and I've been sitting here looking at the stars. They're beautiful tonight."

We look at the stars for a second and then look down.

"Let's go inside," Abba says gruffly.

I shudder as I walk slowly through the door. I don't want to be grounded again. I just want to help people, and keep our village safe . . . and study for my science test.

Chapter 21

In Trouble

"THIS way," Abba says. Like prisoners being led to the guillotine, we slowly follow our father into the living room. He signals for us to sit down on our black leather sofa. We do. He stands in the middle of the room and Ima leans against the doorframe.

Abba shakes his head. "I don't know what to say. I am disappointed in you boys."

We bow our heads. I sway back and forth in my seat. Ziv wipes some tears from his eyes.

"I tried to be good and not worry you about my book," I say hurriedly, looking at Ima. "We didn't want you to be upset. You weren't feeling well. Noam said he could help us. He could make it dark so that no one would see us."

Ima nods like she understands.

"We never expected to see Nadav and Nitzan in—" Ziv clasps his hand over his mouth.

"You are so dumb!" I whisper, throwing up my hands.

Abba and Ima exchange surprised looks. Abba shuts his eyes for a second. I'll bet he's thinking about Mr. Portaal and Nadav.

"I'm going to get some milk for the boys," Ima says quickly. "Ben, will you come and help me?"

Abba nods. "You two stay here," Abba orders us.

As soon as they are gone, Ziv turns to me. "Why didn't you tell Mr. Portaal that Nadav and Nitzan were in the school tonight stealing the test questions?" he whispers fiercely to me.

"I didn't want to squeal on them."

"I thought you didn't like Nadav."

"I don't."

"Then why did you protect him?"

"I don't know!"

"He stole the test. That was bad. You said so yourself."

I clear my throat. "I just thought . . ." I stop. I don't have the words to explain.

When Ima and Abba return from the kitchen, Abba still has his stern face on. He speaks to us in his hard voice. "Jordan and Ziv, Ima and I are unhappy with you."

We sit still, our cheeks flushed.

Abba clears his throat and looks at me, then Ziv, and back to me. "You know your gift and you know Noam's. I assume Noam was responsible for the clap of thunder that scared Ima out of her sleep."

We laugh for a second and then quickly become serious again.

"You have acted childishly and irresponsibly." Abba looks at us through sad eyes. "You were warned not to use these gifts in any way except in an emergency." He pauses and looks at me. "Forgetting your book was not an emergency. Do you understand?"

I nod. I know that now. I also know that I shouldn't have enlisted Ziv and Noam in my little caper. I wipe my eyes on the sleeve of my shirt.

"I agree with Mr. Portaal that you should be punished, so Jordan, I've decided that you will not be allowed to swim in the lake for a month."

I gasp. "A month . . . without going into the lake?" I jump

up from the sofa. "I only just got to go back to the lake after my last punishment!"

Abba nods.

"That's not fair," I yell and run out of the living room. I scramble up the stairs and throw myself on my bed. I beat my pillow with my hands.

"And as for you, Ziv . . . as for you . . ." Abba's angry voice floats up the stairs. There's a pause.

I push my pillow aside, jump off my bed and rush out to the landing. What punishment is Ziv going to get? Guilt clutches at my throat. I got Ziv into this.

"I don't know what kind of punishment you deserve," Abba says.

"Well, how about not letting me go into the lake for a month, like Jordan?"

"No, Ziv. That wouldn't really be a punishment for you." I imagine Abba reaching up and scratching the top of his head like he does when he's thinking. "Your punishment," he says slowly, "is that you will not be allowed in the living room if someone comes to visit us for the next two weeks. You will have to stay in your room if we have company."

"Oh, no!" Ziv gasps. "You know how I like to see the company and their colors."

Abba says nothing.

I see Ziv slowly dragging himself up the stairs. I race into my room and plop down on my bed. The future flashes before my eyes; no lake for a month. I groan. I bang my head hard against my pillow. Ziv got a punishment he hates. Now he's going to hate me. And I still haven't studied for my test and now it's too late and I'm going to fail.

Chapter 22

Meeting Nadav at the Lake

I N the early morning, I sling my backpack over my shoulders and drag myself downstairs.

"Where are you off to this early?" Ima asks from the kitchen.

"I'm going to the lake."

"Remember what Abba said."

I nod. "Of course I remember. He didn't say I couldn't *go* to the lake, did he?"

Ima thinks for a second. "No he didn't forbid you from going to the lake. Just don't get any part of yourself in it."

"Don't worry Ima, I won't."

"How about some breakfast first?" she asks.

I shake my head. The only way I'll clear my head is by looking at the water. I slip out the door and head for the calming waters. Today is going to be my worst day ever at school. A science test I'm going to fail, Mr. Portaal prowling the halls, and no lake privileges. I need to think.

It doesn't take long before I get to the lake. I swat at the tall grass that has grown up all around in the few weeks since the summer. When I'm close to the edge, but not close enough to get wet, I drop my backpack and plop down. I hear the water lapping against the bank, pulling at the little pebbles with a hissing sound. The aching in my head begins to fade. I close my eyes, nodding my head to the rhythm of the water.

Suddenly I hear a splash. My eyes burst open. Nadav, his dark eyes bulging, is standing up to his knees in the lake, staring at me.

"What are you doing?" I ask.

"What's it to you?" he replies sarcastically.

I shrug my shoulders. "I'm just surprised to see you standing there. What are you gonna do about the science test?"

"My dad said there won't be a science test today."

"What?"

"There's going to be a student assembly." Nadav is watching me like I'm a bug under a microscope.

"A student assembly? Why?" I ask.

"My father said that the students of Kfar Keshet are going to decide the punishment of the five boys who broke into the school last night."

"Five boys?" My mouth falls open. "How did he know?"

"I told him," Nadav says. "It was so dumb."

I can't believe Nadav told his father.

"I was home asleep. Abba came home after unlocking the school. He was boiling mad. He slammed the front door and it woke me up, so I went downstairs and he told me the story. Blah, blah, blah . . . Ziv and Jordan are locked in the school. Blah, blah, blah. When I heard you and Ziv were also in the school, I figured you ratted on me. Like an idiot I began to blabber about needing to see the test questions. Then I saw the look on my dad's face. He didn't know what I was talking about." Nadav sighs. "It was too late. I blabbed on myself!" Nadav strikes his forehead with the flat of his palm.

I watch Nadav and don't say anything. He looks less mean when he's sad.

I lean back against a tree trunk. *Bummer*, I'm thinking. *Self-incrimination has really got to hurt.*

"Is there any place here where a person can get sucked under?" Nadav asks, pointing to the lake bottom.

"I don't think so. I know most of the lake and I've never found anything like quicksand. Is that what you mean?"

"Yeah. I thought maybe I could get pulled under . . . or something."

"Naw, don't worry."

"I'm not worried." Nadav looked around and then back at me. "I want to get sucked under and disappear."

I don't know what to say to that. Things must be pretty bad for him. I pick up some stones and toss them one by one into the water.

"Did you come for an early morning swim?" Nadav asks.

"Naw, I can't."

"Can't?"

"I'm being punished. One month – no lake."

"Rough." Nadav wades out of the water, climbs the bank, and sits down in the grass next to me. He swallows a couple of times. I look at him. Now what?

"Listen." He finds his voice. "I feel like . . . like . . . I need to thank you."

"Me?"

Nadav nods. "You didn't rat on me. That was really a brave thing to do." His eerie dark eyes are staring straight into mine, but they don't look as weird to me as they used to.

My face heats up. "Ah, forget it," I say. "I'm sure you would have done the same."

Nadav swallows and stares at his feet. There is a sound of trampling leaves and Nadav looks up. "What's that?" He jumps to his feet and looks around.

"Oh, probably the elves who live in the woods," I joke.

"What elves?" Nadav asks worriedly, looking around.

"Oh, forget it. I was only teasing."

Nadav takes another look into the woods and pulls on his shirt and sandals.

"I guess I'll go to school now," I say, standing up. "You ready?"

"Naw, I'm not going." Nadav shakes his head. "I told my father last night how I felt about this stupid place. I've got to get to Haifa to be with my mom."

"Well, I'll see you," I say.

Nadav waves at me and walks quickly into the woods.

Too bad he's leaving, I'm thinking. We could be friends.

Chapter 23

The Students Decide

AT the school assembly, our faces flushed, our heads down, we hear the punishment the students have decided for us. Two weeks working with old Mr. Handler in the park for Ziv and I. Noam has to work in the library, and Nitzan and Nadav have to help the janitor clean up after school for the next two weeks. My head aches. We won't be able to continue with our jobs at the zoo. We can kiss our extra money good-bye. And how are we going to explain it to Jacob?

"It's okay," Ellah says after the assembly. "You were doing what you thought was right. Right?"

My face heats up and I'm sure it's turned the usual beet red. I can't answer her. I need to get out of here. I bolt down the hall and out the door. I don't care about school; I need to talk to Miss Sara. With my head down, I run past Chaim's guard post. Outside, I take a deep breath and head toward the center of the village. I don't care if they catch me out of school, I'm out of here.

It's market day in the village square. I know where to find Miss Sara. She'll be at her booth under the giant olive tree, selling fabric. As I round the corner, I see her sitting behind the long table covered with her famous, colorful, woven fabric. She's weaving something orange and green on a small, portable loom, her head bent close to her work.

I cross the crowded market square and slump down next to her. I stare at the ground and push some stones with the toe of my shoe. Miss Sara looks up from her work and runs her hand through my hair. Her soft touch makes me feel like I don't have to be ashamed.

"Did you ever notice that some days seem longer than others?" she asks in her quiet voice.

I nod slowly and swipe a hand across my eyes. I'm glad Miss Sara hasn't asked why I'm not in school. Maybe she understands that I needed to get away.

"Was Mr. Portaal hard on you guys?"

"No. I guess he was fair. He let the kids name our punishment."

"What did they decide?"

"They gave all of us, Ziv, Noam, Nadav, Nitzan, and I, public service to do around town."

"Ahh," Miss Sara says softly. "So it was Nadav who locked you in the school."

"I thought you knew," I say, looking up. "Nadav and Nitzan were in the school when we were."

"Nadav and Nitzan were in the school?"

I shrug.

"What were they doing there?"

"Nadav was looking for the test questions."

"Oh my gosh!" Miss Sara seems really surprised. "He went to steal the test?"

I nod. I think I can tell now. Everyone knows he was in the school.

"Mr. Portaal must have been really upset knowing his own son was trying to steal the test questions." She makes a tsk tsk sound. "How did the students know who did it? Didn't Mr. Portaal try to keep your names secret?"

"When Mr. Portaal started talking, Ziv got all teary-eyed and Noam started to cry. I tried to look like I wasn't involved, but my face turned beet red. Everyone guessed right away."

"What did Nadav do? He must have been totally embarrassed."

"He wasn't there. I met him down at the lake before school started. He said he wasn't going to school."

"Oh, dear, he's having a hard time adjusting to Kfar Keshet." Miss Sara sighs deeply.

"He told me he hates it here."

"That's too bad. We could be so good for him."

I shrug. I don't care anymore. All I can think about is that for the next two weeks, Ziv and I have to clean the parks and help Mr. Handler paint the playground equipment. No work at the zoo and no extra money.

Miss Sara rubs her chin and weaves in a steady rhythm.

"Hey, Jordan!"

I look over my shoulder. It's Ziv. School must be over. He walks over and sits down. "Hi, Miss Sara. Did you hear? We got a punishment from the kids at school."

Miss Sara nods. "Two weeks working at the park. That's not so bad. Why do you think Nadav took Nitzan?"

"Maybe Nadav was afraid to be in the school by himself," Ziv suggests.

"Are you kidding?" I groan. "Nadav isn't afraid of anything."

I've thought about it myself, though. Why *did* Nadav bring Nitzan? Why have a witness? Was he trying to make Nitzan his friend? Does Nitzan owe him something? I have no idea.

Chapter 24

Helping Mr. Handler

A S Ziv and I enter the zoo we see Jacob and Mordechai working in Aish's cage.

"You guys are late," Jacob says, without looking up from the straw-filled floor. "Let's get to work."

"Um . . . we can't work for you for a while," I gulp.

"What? Why not?"

"I guess you didn't hear. Ziv and I are being punished for breaking into the school last night. We've got community service. Two weeks with Mr. Handler in the gardens every afternoon after school." I bite my lip.

"While you work with Mr. Handler, what am I supposed to do? I need you two here."

"We're sorry, Jacob. We really liked working for you, and the money and all, but we're being punished, we have no choice," I explain.

"This is no good," Jacob sighs. "I'll have to get a new worker."

"We'd kind of like to pet some of the animals, if you don't mind," Ziv asks.

"Sure, go ahead. Just remember . . . lock the cage doors when you're finished."

Ziv's face turns red.

"No problem," I say and push Ziv forward.

After petting the three-headed dog and some of the other animals at the zoo, we go meet Mr. Handler at the center of the village.

"Well, well, who do we have here?" Mr. Handler booms at us in greeting. On his bald head he's wearing a floppy straw hat, and his legs are clothed in grass-stained jeans. He points to a small red brick hut tucked into the corner of the community garden. "Welcome to Kfar Keshet's tool shed. This is where we keep all the tools, paints, and brushes that we use in the gardens."

The shed is overgrown with crawling ivy vines and looks like a cottage out of Hansel and Gretel. As Mr. Handler heaves open the creaky wooden door, an odor of dampness and fertilizer seeps out. "Come on in," he urges. "Nothing's going to bite you."

Slowly, we follow the big man inside.

Garden tools lie all over the dirt floor, all jumbled up. A rough wooden table stands against the far wall. A number of dark bottles and jars filled with plant vitamins and insecticides cover its surface. Under the window there are red plastic buckets covered with large splotches of green paint. What a mess, I'm thinking. I hope he's not going to make us clean this up.

"Today we're going to trim the gooseberry bushes. Grab a pair of shears and follow me."

We hunt around the hut until we find two pairs of shears. Then we step outside and trail after Mr. Handler. It is hours later when we return our shears to a corner in the shed and step outside.

"Look at this crud," Ziv complains, using a stick to scrape off the mud caked on his shoes. "Gardens are really dirty places."

"Just like at the zoo. Remember how filthy it was the first few days? Then we got used to it," I remind him.

"Yeah, but we didn't get all splattered with mud there. Trimming bushes is really dirtifying."

"Hey, I like your new word!"

Ziv frowns. I guess he doesn't think it's that funny.

I sigh. "I know what you mean, though. I'd like to go jump into the lake. This dirt would float away in a second." I look hungrily in the direction of the lake.

"Forget it. You remember what Abba said. You've got a whole month to think about jumping in."

"Darn!" I kick at some small pebbles.

"Noam sure got off easy. Two weeks in the library isn't such a bad job. Maybe he'd like to switch," Ziv says. "Let's go ask him."

"First, we have to get this muck off our shoes and clothes. Let's go home."

While we're walking home, I'm thinking about my life for the next few weeks. School from eight till three, afternoons with Mr. Handler, evenings studying science, English, and government. No lake, no swimming, no time to just read a book, find out about golems, or help people.

Chapter 25

A Trip to the Library

AFTER a cold glass of our favorite drink, *limonana* – lemonade with mint –and a generous helping of chocolate chip cookies, we leave home and head for the library. As we enter, cool air-conditioned air envelops us. The bright sunlight remains outside, and for a few moments it's hard to see. When our eyes adjust we catch sight of Noam walking toward the fiction section, pushing a rubber-wheeled cart.

"Hey, Noam! It certainly is nice and cool in here," I call.

Noam turns and waves. "I haven't been out all day," he complains. "Not a chance to see the cloud formations or anything. This is a terrible punishment."

Ziv and I exchange surprised looks. We hadn't thought about that aspect of Noam's punishment.

"We've been out looking at the clouds all day," I say. I show Noam the dirt under my fingernails that I tried to scrub off for about an hour. "That's what kids get when they work outside."

"You wanna trade?" Noam asks.

"That's a great idea," I say. "I'd love to work in the library."

Shoshana, the hawk-eyed librarian sitting at the counter, raises a finger to her lips. "Shush!"

"Follow me," Noam says in a whisper. He pushes the loaded cart toward the far right side of the library into the science section. He stops at the end of an aisle and leans against a bookshelf.

We hear a familiar voice. "You're in my favorite section of the library. I love books on spiders."

"Hi, Ellah." I smile.

"Having a powwow or something?" she asks.

Noam frowns. "It's none of your business," he says.

"I thought I'd look up some books on golems," Ellah says. "But if you're not interested . . ."

"That's a great idea," I say quickly.

"Yeah, good idea, Ella," Ziv says.

"This is a library, not a clubhouse." We turn around. Shoshana the librarian is frowning at us through the books.

"Oops, sorry," I say. "We were just wondering if there are any books about golems."

The librarian's brown eyes open wide. "Golems? Is this for school? That's kind of an unusual subject."

"Well, it's not exactly for school. We—"

Ellah elbows me in the back and says, "We're thinking of using the information for a report."

"Let's see what books we have," the librarian says as she moves toward the computer terminal. "But be quiet about it."

"Get a load of this," I say in my quiet voice when Ellah and Ziv sit down next to me. The table is stacked high with books the librarian helped us find. "There are a million books on golems."

"Gee." Ziv exhales. He leafs through a couple of books.

Shoshana glares at us from her desk.

"Shhh," I warn my friends.

"Look at this," Ellah says, pointing to a familiar picture. "It's Frankenstein. He was a golem."

Ziv grabs the book and turns it around to see the picture.

Ellah picks up her notebook and reads us a list of golem traits from her notes:

They have a word written on their forehead.
They either don't speak at all, or very little.
They are created to help the person who created them.
They don't have souls.
They usually need to be destroyed because they turn on their master.

"So how . . . how can they be destroyed?" Ziv's voice shakes as he asks the most important question of all.

"It kind of depends. You've got to take a letter off the word written on their forehead," Ellah says.

"How do you do that?" I ask.

⚹ ⚹ ⚹

That night, golems keep running through my mind. I lay my head down, punch my pillow, bunch up my sheets, throw off my blanket, and wait to fall asleep. After a while my bed seems to be swaying like it's floating on water. Oops, I better not be on the lake. Dad will kill me. I hold on to my bed as it floats off over the dam. Splash! It lands in the lake. This bed is going backwards. If you fall off the dam, you land in the river. Where am I going? The bed drifts past a campfire on the shore. A ragged man in a white dress is kneeling at the water's edge.

I pull the sheet over my head. Then I'm rippling like water, swirling around the strange man. The man throws a bucket into the water. I slither into the bucket and I'm pulled out of the water. With a splash, I land on the bank. The man smiles down at me and points a glowing yellow finger at my forehead. I raise my hands to protect myself, but my hands are water. The nail on his yellow finger spins in circles like a drill. Closer and closer it comes to my forehead. "Help," I yell, or try to. The eddy of air rushing off the fingernail drill sends a chill down my spine. "Help, help, he's going to write something on my forehead. Help, helllllp!"

"Wake up, Jordan." Ziv is tugging at my arm. "Wake up! You're having a nightmare."

I shoot up in bed. "He almost did it. He almost did it."

"Did what?" Ziv asks.

"He almost branded me on my forehead. It was Lavan, the man who made the golem."

"Go back to sleep, Jordan. You read too many golem books today."

I sink back into my warm covers and lie still, waiting for my racing heart to settle down.

Chapter 26

A Visit to the Zoo

THE next day, after working in the community garden with Mr. Handler, I say, "Let's go to the zoo."

"Great idea," Ziv says. "I miss the animals."

"I'm curious about Mordechai."

"Still?" Ziv asks.

"He could be the golem."

We turn up the street and head toward Jacob's zoo. When we pass Mr. Portaal's house, Ziv asks, "Have you seen Nadav at all? He like . . . disappeared."

"He told me he wasn't going back to school. Maybe he went to his mom in Haifa," I say.

"I guess that's better than staying with his angry old man."

The zoo looks pretty much the same as the day before, except a new cage has been added. Inside the cage is a pink and white striped kitten that looks like a candy cane.

"They must have read Eden a goose-bumpy story," I say.

"Isn't she cute?" Ziv steps toward the cage.

The cat snarls, and Ziv jumps back hastily. "Bad temper," he says. "Let's visit the others."

Jacob approaches us from the tool shed carrying a large

metal rake. "Are you two looking for a job?" he asks with a smile.

"Naw, not yet, unfortunately. We just came by to see the animals and say hello."

"I guess you saw Eden's latest creation." Jacob points at the fuzzy little pink and white kitten curled up in a ball. "She's pretty as a picture but mean as a hornet. Somehow Eden put that combination together. Not sure where she got the idea . . ."

"Someone's going to get a finger bitten off," Ziv grumbles.

"Not to worry. We try to keep down the number of visitors," Jacob says.

"How's it going?" I ask.

Jacob takes off his baseball cap and swipes the sweat from his forehead. "I've got a new worker and he's turned out just fine."

"That's good. Is Mordechai still working with you, too?" I ask.

"Yeah."

"Great. The animals like him."

Jacob nods. "And he's great with Eden, too. Well, I'm off to my chores," he says. "Go do some petting. I'm sure the animals will be glad to see you two." Jacob hoists his rake over his shoulder and marches off.

We wind our way among the cages. We pat each of the heads of the three-headed dog and hold some straw up for Aish to set on fire. We kneel down next to the ape-cheetah and scratch his ears.

"What did Jacob mean about Mordechai being great with Eden?" I wonder aloud. "If he's the golem, Eden could really be in trouble."

"Maybe he's just an ordinary guy," Ziv suggests.

"Maybe."

As we near the front gate, Jacob, Mordechai, and another man are standing in a circle talking. We edge toward them.

"Who is that?" Ziv whispers.

I stare. "It must be that new hand Jacob hired, but I can't make out who it is."

We move closer. We're always suspicious of new people. Unfortunately, we can't see who the new worker is. The men disappear into the feed shack.

"Let's get out of here," Ziv says.

I nod and we hurry out of the zoo and head for home.

*　*　*

I lie in bed. My muscles are still aching from the work I did cutting off the large limbs of the linden trees in the park. As I get comfortable in my bed I wonder how someone might remove a letter from a person's forehead. Maybe you just use an eraser? But the word has been tattooed into the skin. Maybe a nail file or exfoliation cream? Weird ideas float through my head. I punch my pillow for the thousandth time and yawn mightily. There's got to be a way.

Chapter 27

At the Zoo

"YOU'VE done a great job." Mr. Handler smiles and shakes our hands. "The two weeks have passed so quickly."

What? He thinks the two weeks passed quickly? I exchange a strained look with Ziv.

"What do you plan to do with your time now?" Mr. Handler asks.

"We were working at the zoo before. I think we're going to go back and see if Jacob still needs our help," I say.

"Well, good luck to you two, and don't go breaking into the school again."

I clench my fists. Then I drop them to my side. "Thanks," I say coolly. Mr. Handler nods and gives us his friendly smile and heads for the shack.

"Let's go to the zoo," I say to Ziv as we put away the rakes.

"Not me," Ziv says. "I'm going to meet up with Noam. He's finishing in the library. I told him I'd meet him there."

"No problem. See you later." I wave good-bye.

Deep in thought, I meander toward the zoo. I keep remembering the dream I had the other night. The memory of the man in white sends shivers up my spine. Is he after me?

I arrive at the zoo and wander aimlessly, staring at the animals without really seeing them. I pass Aish's cage, but don't throw any twigs at him. I wave at the three-headed dog without patting its heads. There's a commotion coming

from the pink and white striped kitten's cage, but it takes several moments before I realize that's where it's coming from. My ears perk up when I hear the kitten's deep snarls.

I run quickly toward the noise, then screech to a halt. Eden is inside the cage, backed into a corner. The cat is planted in front of Eden, snarling and spitting at two men fighting each other.

Cold fingers clutch my throat. I stand rooted to the ground as indecision floods my brain. I can guess who the men are, but I can't tell which is which. They look so similar. Like twins.

"Don't fight! Don't fight!" Eden is screaming in a quivery voice.

I lunge forward. Grabbing a shovel I see on the ground, I push open the cage door.

"Stop!" I yell.

The two men stop. They turn and face me for a moment. I blink wildly and look from one to the other. One is Mordechai and the other is Chaim. Like I thought. Both have caps tight over their foreheads. Why are they fighting? Which one is the golem?

Chaim runs toward me. He grabs the shovel from me and pushes me to the ground, then twirls and faces Mordechai. As I watch from where I'm lying, he raises the shovel and smacks Mordechai on the shoulder. Mordechai pitches forward and falls on me. His baseball cap flies off, but before I can get a good look at his forehead, Chaim pounces on me. He slaps me on the ear. My head ringing, I roll over, holding my ear, but I still manage to keep my eye on the men.

Mordechai wobbles to his feet, lowers his head, and butts Chaim in the stomach. Chaim falls, landing on his back, and his cap falls off. I squint. There is something on Chaim's forehead, but I can't see what it is.

"Daddy, Daddy, help me, help me!" Eden is screaming.

Mordechai is leaning against the bars of the cage, breathing heavily. I stare at his forehead and see a jagged scar. That explains why he wears his baseball cap all the time.

I see Chaim's cap lying on the floor. I lunge forward and grab it. Chaim gropes on the ground, searching for his cap. He looks up at me with angry eyes and I see the word

DREAD on his sweaty forehead. He throws his hands over his forehead and roars.

He must be the golem. He starts to move slowly to his feet, clenching and unclenching his hands. He's going to wring my neck.

I step backwards. My shoulder hits the bars of the cage. I'm trapped. Chaim lunges forward, and grabs me by the neck of my tee shirt. He lifts me off the ground by my neck. Stars erupt before my eyes.

Just then, Jacob rushes toward us. "What's happening here?" he yells.

Chaim opens his gigantic hands and drops me to the ground. I breathe deep, jagged breaths.

"Daddy, Daddy, help!" Eden cries.

The pink and white cat, still planted in front of her, snarls ferociously. Its fur is sticking out in spikes.

"It's just a misunderstanding," Mordechai says. He rises slowly to his feet, shoving his hat back over his scar.

"I just wanted to take Eden for a little ride on my bike, and Mordechai started to act strange," Chaim says as he sits on the ground holding his stomach. He's pulled his cap on again so we can't see his forehead.

I shake my head to clear the ringing in my ears.

"Come to me, Eden," Jacob says, holding out his hands.

Eden sidles around the angry kitten and throws herself into her father's arms. "Stay where you are," Jacob orders the men. We're going to get to the bottom of this." Jacob's eyes blaze. His face is beet red. He spits on the floor and then looks at the men. "You two endangered my daughter. Are you crazy?" He turns to me. "Jordan, is that you? What are you doing here?"

I give a slight wave of my hand. I can't speak yet.

"I'm taking Eden home. You two stay right here. I'll call Sergeant Freed if I have to. I'll be right back. You two have a lot of explaining to do." Jacob leaves the cage, his arms wrapped around Eden.

I've got to get out of here. I slowly crawl to the cage door, and, as I reach it, the kitten lets out a great big howl. It startles everyone, and distracts Chaim and Mordechai from what I'm doing. I escape through the door and scurry behind a neighboring cage. Then I carefully pick my way past the remaining cages to the exit and sneak out of the zoo. My arms and legs are shaking. I feel stunned, but have only one thought. I've got to see Miss Sara. I need to tell her about Chaim and the tattoo on his forehead. He must be the golem.

Chapter 28

Escape from the Zoo

RUN down the avenue toward Miss Sara's street as fast as I can manage. Sput, sput. I hear a motorcycle start up. Chaim is after me on his Yamaha. I've got to hide. I dash across Bar Kochba street and hide in the bushes opposite the fire station. I keep my head tucked low to my chest. Hardly breathing, I listen for the motorcycle to pass.

"Jordan, Jordan, where are you? I can explain everything." It's Chaim's voice.

I look back. At the corner I can see Chaim moving slowly toward my hiding place. He's looking carefully behind every fence and tree. Shivering with fear, I inch further along the hedge. I saw the tattoo. I think Chaim is the golem. This is my chance to catch him. I'll use my gift. Indecision wraps its icy fingers around my heart. Would this be using my gift for the right thing? I'd be protecting Kfar Keshet. It has to be right.

I have an idea. There's a break in the greenery up ahead. I'll step out on the sidewalk so I can see Chaim and I'll crash him with a tsunami wave. While he's lying there, I'll flow to Miss Sara's house, get a rope, and tie him up. The idea is perfect. I clap my hands.

I step out from behind the green bushes. My heart is

beating a hole in my chest. Chaim sees me. The motorcycle speeds up. Its roar fills the air. I try to repeat my words but I can't think. Flow, blow . . . nothing. He's gaining on me. I start again. He's almost on top of me. Flow, blow, roll. I repeat my mantra a couple of times. Then, suddenly, instead of a huge tsunami I'm a small puddle of water spurted out on the street.

Puzzled, Chaim screeches his motorcycle to a stop. He jumps down and slowly turns his head, searching for me up and down the street. He clomps behind the bushes and heads for the forest, leaving his motorcycle by the side of the road. After what feels like an hour, he returns. He steps over the puddle that's me. For a brief moment he bends down to look at the water. I feel his eyes on me. Then he stands up and walks towards his motorcycle. I hear him rev his bike and start to move off.

I wait another fraction of a minute and then re-form. I run as fast as I can in the direction of Miss Sara's house. I hear heavy feet tramping the dried leaves behind me. I duck behind a tree and look back. It's Chaim. I run faster. He's gaining on me. I can feel his hot breath on my neck. Without even thinking about it, my mantra fills my head. His hand reaches out to grab me but I splash out of his reach.

Chapter 29

Miss Sara Solves the Puzzle

I FLOW over grass and pebbles through the forest to Miss Sara's house. She is tending her sheep in the pasture in front of her house.

I reconfigure myself as quickly as I can.

"Miss Sara," I pant in a ragged voice.

She sees me and hurries through the gate to greet me. "What happened?"

I feel flushed. I'm shaking and I bend over to catch my breath. Then I straighten up and smile weakly. "I saw his forehead . . ." I wipe a dribble of water from my forehead and hold my damaged ear for a second. "There's a word on Chaim's forehead—"

"Slow down," Miss Sara says as she pats my arm. "Follow me."

We go inside and walk to her kitchen. She points me to a seat at the table. Then she fills a glass with a pale green liquid, and hands it to me. "Drink this slowly," she says. She sits down opposite me, watching me closely.

With shaky hands I raise the glass and drink in noisy gulps. A weird lime and pepper taste fills my mouth. I put the glass down.

"Okay, now tell me slowly what you saw," Miss Sara says.

"I saw the two men." I gulp. "Mordechai and Chaim."

"I know about the two men. Just tell me what you saw."

"They were fighting each other and their caps fell off. On Mordechai's forehead there was a jagged scar. That's why he wears a baseball cap."

Miss Sara nods like she's known that all along.

"And on Chaim's forehead—" Miss Sara urges. "What word was there?"

"I saw the word DREAD." I sit back in the chair, exhausted.

Miss Sara pushes back her chair and rushes to her writing desk. "Thank you, Jordan. You did great," she says warmly.

"No," I say. "I tried to stop him and I failed."

Miss Sara says nothing. I watch her pull open the top drawer, lift out a pen and paper, and return to her seat across from me. She looks at me intently. "When you read the books about golems at the library, do you remember what they said? How you destroy them?"

I think for a moment and then nod. "I remember reading something about erasing one letter from the forehead to change the word written there and make the golem return to its original form."

Miss Sara smiles approvingly. "Yes, that's correct. Now look at this tattoo. Can you figure out what letter should be erased?"

I turn the paper around. I stare silently at it. Suddenly my mouth falls open. "Of course, that's it. It's so simple. If I remove the "R" from the word DREAD it becomes the work DEAD." I breathe out, stunned.

Miss Sara nods.

"But how do we erase the letter?" I ask.

"That's not so easy. We'll have to look it up in the book."

I follow Miss Sara into her office. She lifts the big green book from the shelf, then thumbs through the index until she finds what she's looking for. She licks her finger and begins to flip the pages. I lean forward to get a better look. She turns almost to the end of the book. On one of the last pages, she opens the book wide, scanning the page.

She narrows her eyes at me. "It's not going to be easy."

My heart is beating out the rhythm of a jackhammer. "Wha . . . what do I have to do?" I ask. I can do it, I tell myself, whatever it is.

"Look, it's illustrated right here." Miss Sara points to the bottom of the page.

I lean over the thick book. Five drawings indicate what we have to do.

I see a small drawing of a worm. Next to that is a drawing of a hand holding the worm over a word written on someone's forehead. The third picture shows the worm stretched out on the letter, oozing a liquid. The second to the last illustration shows a hand picking up the now dead worm and tossing it. The last picture shows that the letter has disappeared from the forehead.

"That's all there is to it," Miss Sara says, her voice shaking.

"Where do I get this type of worm?" I gulp.

"They're in the lake where the golem was created. These worms are leftover pieces of dirt that Lavan blessed but didn't become part of the golem. They've become aquatic worms. They are segmented and have very thin skins. They live very far down, all the way at the bottom of the lake."

I'm shaking my head. Slimy, skinny worms at the bottom of the lake . I feel a wad of food rising in my throat. "You need to reunite at least one of the worms with the golem," Miss Sara says.

"I don't think I can swim that deep."

"I don't think so, either. You'll have to use your gift and become water, dive down, pick up one or two of the worms, and bring them to the surface."

"That's fine, but when I become like water I don't have hands. How do I pick them up?"

"I guess you'll have to pick them up in your mouth, dear. You do have a mouth while you're water, right?"

I think about this. I don't have a mouth every time. I did when I rescued Ziv. When I'm using my gift in a forceful way, like a tsunami, I don't have a mouth. When I'm using it to help someone, I do.

"You'll have to carry them in your mouth with water so they don't dry out. They dry out easily."

The thought makes my face turn green. I rub the back of my neck. "Isn't there any other way?"

"I don't think so, dear. That's what's written here. We have the worms at the bottom of the lake. You just have to bring them up, keep them wet, find the golem, and lay one on the letter. The worm will do the rest."

"Why do we have to bring the golem to the lake? I could just fish out one of those worms, find the golem and drop it on his head."

Miss Sara shakes her head. "The worm must remain in the lake water until the moment you scoop it out and put it on the golem's head."

I could take some water out of the lake in a bowl and keep the worm in it," I say.

"It has to be living water. When you dip out the water it loses that quality. "Jordan, you've got your gift. This will be easy. So you'll only bring up one worm, not two. Is that better?"

I shrug my shoulders.

"Why did Lavan name the golem Chaim? Chaim means life," I say.

Miss Sara shakes her head. "Just one of Lavan's ironic little jokes, I imagine. He creates a golem who has no soul and is really like something dead, and calls it 'life'."

I stand up. My nerves are all jiggly and my sweaty shirt

is stuck to my back. I pace around the desk, then inch my way back to the book and study the pictures once more. Flopping back into the chair, I lower my head onto the table.

Miss Sara frowns. "You can do this, Jordan. Kfar Keshet is depending on you."

I cross my arms over my head as if I can hide from the visions of worms swimming down my throat. I feel nauseous.

"Tomorrow night is the full moon. Just like the night when he was created. We have to bring him back to the place of his creation. The only hard part will be getting the golem to the lake. Do you know how to get him there?"

I shake my head. My brain is a frozen ice cube.

"We'll meet here tomorrow and come up with a plan," I hear Miss Sara say before I stumble out of her house.

Chapter 30

Get the Golem to the Lake

THE golem . . . the lake . . . thoughts spin around in my mind like a whirlpool as I trudge along the tree-lined path. How do I get the golem to the lake? Who can help me? My thoughts keep hitting a brick wall. As I walk past the giant olive tree in the center of town, I hear someone whistle.

Frowning as my thoughts slither away, I look around. Is it Mordechai or Chaim hunting for me? My heart begins racing. I look over my shoulder. No one is there. It's twilight. The square seems empty. Annoyed, I kick at a loose pebble. As it bounces away I hear the whistle again. It's coming from the olive tree. I look up. Nadav is sitting in the thick branches.

I rub my eyes. It's really Nadav. No one has seen him for two and a half weeks.

"Come on up," Nadav says, and pats a limb next to the one he's perched on.

"I'm busy," I say.

"I've got some private info you need," Nadav says.

I shrug. "I think I've got enough information for one day."

"Don't be dumb. What's the matter? You only swim, you don't climb trees?"

I shrug, grab a low limb, and hoist myself up into the tree. I clamber up, branch over branch, and squat next to Nadav.

"You know I climb trees, too," I say under my breath. "What have you got?"

I pick an unripe olive from the tree and throw it at the Kfar Keshet sign below us. It hits the sign and bounces off with a little twang.

Nadav shifts on his branch. He peers directly at me with his dark eyes. "I know who the golem is." He smiles smugly.

How does he know about the golem, I'm wondering. Someone must have told him. It wasn't me. Why is he talking about him now?

"So?" I pick off another olive and aim it at the sign.

"So . . . I'm back from two weeks with my mother. All I hear is golem, golem, golem. All you guys are trying to figure out who the golem is, and I know. I thought I'd tell you as a thank you for not squealing on me."

"Don't bother." I exhale. "I know who the golem is, too." But what I'm thinking is, who did he hear from?

Nadav's eyes widen. "You do? I thought I was the only one."

"Nope, there are two of us."

"Oh." Nadav's shoulders sag and he stares down at the grass.

I nod and sit silently in the tree for a moment, tossing a new thought around. Then I say slowly, "Nadav, I know you've been kind of pals with Chaim. I remember seeing you riding on his Yamaha."

Nadav doesn't answer right away. Then he says, "He seemed so quiet. I figured he was lonely . . . and I really liked his motorcycle."

I sit on my branch and plunk olives at the welcome sign.

Nadav turns and stares at me with his black eyes. "I didn't know he was a golem until just now. Yesterday, we drove the motorcycle out to this big old house, past the woods and the border of Kfar Keshet. Guess who we went to see? His 'father,' Lavan, the crazy man. Chaim made me wait outside."

My hair stands on end as I listen to Nadav. He knows where Lavan lives.

Then Nadav says, "Through the window I heard Lavan call Chaim, 'my grand old golem.' All the way home, I was wondering what a golem was, so when I got home I looked up the word on the internet. That's how I found out. Creepy!"

In the gathering dusk I can see Nadav's satisfied grin. I'm thinking of our plan to destroy the golem and the problem of getting him back to the lake.

"If you told the golem to go some place, would he obey you?"

"Of course," Nadav says, sitting up straighter. "We're pals. I'll tell him we're going to have a party. I'll tell him I'm inviting some of the 'gifted kids.' He should like that. He doesn't know that I know his secret."

"Yes!" I clap my hands and punch the air in triumph. The branch I'm sitting on begins to rock, and I grab it with both hands. "Follow me," I say, and I slide out of the tree.

"Where are we going?"

"Well, we need to go to Miss Sara's house, but it's late and my mom will be wondering where I am. I have to run home first and check-in with her. She always wants to know when we'll be home for dinner. Ever since the break-in at the school my folks watch over me like two bloodhounds."

Nadav snickers. "I'll meet you at Miss Sara's in half an hour."

We give each other a high five. Nadav and I working together. What a surprise!

Thirty minutes later, a little after seven, I meet Nadav

outside Miss Sara's house. She answers our knock at her door.

"Long time no see," she says to me. Then she sees Nadav. "I guess I can say the same to you. Come in."

Nadav and I enter and follow Miss Sara into the living room. We sit down on the sofa. Miss Sara adjusts her skirt and sits down in her rocking chair.

"Well?" she asks.

"I've found the way to get the golem to the lake," I say, jumping up from the sofa and jiggling my hips in a celebration dance.

Miss Sara leans forward and eyes Nadav. "I assume this has something to do with you, Nadav, and your relationship with Chaim."

Nadav's face turns reds. We both nod.

"Okay, how are you going to do it?"

I sit down and lean forward. "Nadav is going to invite the golem to go to the lake."

"Nadav, will Chaim want to go with you to the lake?" Miss Sara looks worried.

"Yeah, he thinks I'm organizing a party for him. I'll tell him Nurse Emunah's going to be there."

"Isn't it a great plan? I'll meet them at the lake after I capture a worm, and that will be that." I snap my fingers.

"What worm?" Nadav asks.

"I didn't get to that yet," I say. "Miss Sara, can we show Nadav the pictures in the book?"

Miss Sara nods. She rises from her rocker and heads for her study. Nadav and I follow her. I'm smiling. Nadav and I working together makes me feel like I just aced a science test. Maybe we'll be friends one day. Together, I think we can catch the golem. We have to save the village from Lavan's evil plans.

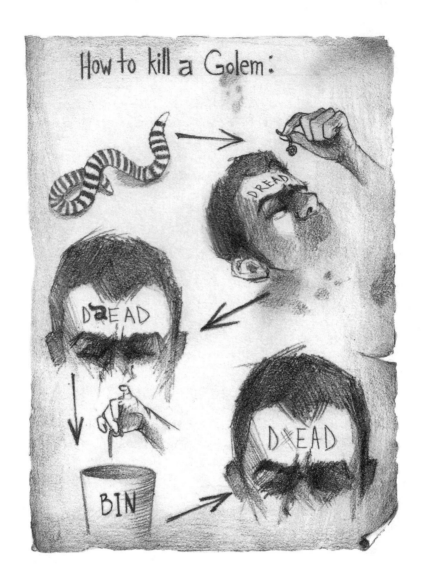

Chapter 31

The Plan

"NOW I understand," Nadav says, fingering the page with the worm drawings. "You need to catch the worm and I need to bring the golem. How are we going to get him to lie down?"

I scratch my head. "Maybe if we had a blanket and pillow we could put him to sleep."

Miss Sara and Nadav shake their heads.

"Just kidding. How about a strong drink? That would make him tipsy and tired," I say.

"The golem doesn't drink alcohol," Miss Sara says.

"Well, what can we do? Hit him over the head?" I pace Miss Sara's living room.

"If we had a big net we could catch him, wrap him in it, lay him down, and put the worm on the letter," Nadav offers.

"A large net . . ." I hop up from my seat. "Ellah weaves nets. Maybe she has one or she'll make us one."

"We haven't got a lot of time," Miss Sara points out. "You two run over to Ellah's house and see if she has something you can use. I'll consult my concoction book and search for some kind of formula that will make the golem drowsy. Things will be a lot easier if you don't have to fight with him too much. I know he's quite strong. His energy is from Lavan."

When we arrive at Ellah's house, we find Noam in the garden polishing the lens on his telescope. When he hears the sound of our footsteps, he spots us.

"Nadav, is that really you?"

"Yep."

"Welcome back," Noam says coolly. "We thought you were gone for good."

"Here I am. It's a long story. I'll tell you about it some-time," Nadav says.

"Where is Ellah?" I ask. My ears and neck are as hot as hothouse tomatoes.

"I dunno, probably in her room. Should I call her?"

Nadav and I nod.

"Elllllllaaaah, there's someone here to see yooouuuu."

A window shoots up and Ellah puts her head out. She waves at me.

"I'll be right down," she shouts and lowers the window.

After a minute or so, Ellah pushes open the back door and steps outside. She walks briskly toward us.

"Nadav, what are you doing here?" she asks without say-ing hello. She doesn't smile.

"It's a long story," Nadav repeats himself. He holds his hands up as if to stop further questions. "I'll tell you one of these days. Right now we're looking for a man-sized net."

"A man-sized net," Ellah repeats. "What would you want with that? Are you going to catch a man?" Ellah pauses. "Or a golem?"

I look at Nadav. He shakes his head almost impercepti-bly. I guess he's thinking without Noam and Ellah's help he'll be the hero and make everyone like him. Ellah, Ziv, and Noam have been part of this. It's not fair to keep them out but I don't know what to do.

"Er . . . we just said 'man-sized' to give you the idea it's for something big," I manage to say.

"What's it for?" Ellah persists. She walks closer and stares at me. "You can tell me."

I feel a little dizzy. My hands hang limply at my sides. I hesitate. "It's a secret," I whisper into her ear. "I'll tell you later."

Ellah stares me down for a moment and then turns to Nadav and says, "I'll tell you what. Come up to my room and I'll show you what I've got. If one is big enough for your purpose, great. If not, I'll make you one tonight."

I sigh with relief and nod. Nadav flashes a smile. We follow her into the house.

Chapter 32

A Net the Size of a Man

'VE never been in Ellah's room before. I'm glad Nadav is with me so I don't feel so awkward. There are woven nets hanging everywhere – over her lamp, hooked on the walls, dangling from the ceiling, draped over pictures of spiders. The nets fill every empty space.

Ellah opens a closet door. Inside I see a shelf full of dozens of mesh woven bags in a hundred different colors. Ellah begins to pull them off the shelf one by one. "I know there's a really big one in here somewhere. Let's see," she says. "I think it's dark brown and green. I remember working on it and I liked it so much it just got bigger and bigger."

Nadav and I start helping Ellah pull out the nets. We drape them on Ellah's bed. When we run out of space we start piling them on her desk.

"Here's a big one," I say, holding up a large brown and green webbed bag. "Is this the one you meant, Ellah? It looks pretty big." I open the bag, sling it over Nadav's head and tug it down to his feet. It completely encases him and there's even room to spare. "Perfect!"

Nadav clears his throat. "Is it strong enough?"

I finger the mesh netting that surrounds him and turn to Ellah. "Yeah, is it?"

"Haven't you ever heard about the strength of spider webs?" asks Ellah. "Wikipedia says that the tensile strength of spider silk is greater than the equivalent weight of steel."

"Perfect!" I grab Ellah's hand and dance her around the room. She grins. By the time we stop we're both blushing. "Oops, sorry I was just . . . just so excited and I . . ."

Ellah nods at me and I stop blabbering.

Ellah gets serious. "Are you two going to tell me what's going on?"

I look at Nadav. Then I lean over and whisper in Ellah's ear. "We're going golem hunting."

Ellah claps her hands. "Then I'm coming too," she says.

"No way," Nadav blurts out.

Ellah glares. "Why not?"

"It's too dangerous and girls always get in the way," Nadav says.

Ellah grabs the web sack surrounding Nadav with two hands. She jerks it quickly and Nadav falls to the floor.

"Hey, how did you do that?" I ask, as I pull the sack off Nadav.

"Part of my spider studies," Ellah gloats.

"Maybe we can use her," I whisper to Nadav.

"You gonna take everyone? It's not a tea party," Nadav hisses.

"I told Ziv when I went home. He's coming, too, to hold on to the worm."

"What worm?" Ellah asks. "I've made some really small bags to hold guppies and things like that. Do you need one of those, too?"

She hands me a very finely woven, tiny bag.

I finger it. "Yep, we need one of these, too. Ziv will keep the worm in this bag, suspended in the lake, until we need it."

Ellah pulls it away from me. "Only if I get to go."

I shrug. It's only fair if she provides the bags, I figure. "Okay, we'll all meet tomorrow morning at Miss Sara's house to plan."

I roll up the two net bags, and Nadav and I head for the door.

"Hey, help me put these nets back," Ellah orders. "If my mom sees this mess I'll be grounded until seventh grade."

Chapter 33

The Team Gathers

THE following morning, Thursday, is the first day of a nice long school vacation, because of the Jewish festival of Succot which begins at sundown and lasts for eight whole days. Each family builds a small hut, a *succah*, outside of their house, to have meals in and even sleep in. Everyone in the family helps build and decorate it. Ziv and I are very proud of our *succah*. After we finish putting up the decorations in our *succah*, Ziv and I meet up with Ellah and Noam and walk over to Miss Sara's house.

"Where is Nadav?" Miss Sara asks.

We all look around.

"Yeah, where is Nadav?" Ziv asks.

I shrug. "He knew we were meeting here this morning. He said he'd be here. I don't know what's happened to him."

"Are you sure we can trust him?" Ziv asks.

I hesitate. "I think so."

"He could be warning the golem right now." Noam paces the floor. "Maybe he's working for Lavan and just stringing us along."

"I think he's okay. I'm sure he'll be here." But I clench my fists and look out the window. The path is empty. I'm not sure why I trust him. Everyone's involved in this because of me. I don't want anything to go wrong, not when we're facing a creature like Lavan.

"I don't have any doubts about Nadav," Miss Sara says.

I breathe a sigh of relief.

Ziv and Noam grumble something that I can't hear.

"Look, here he is," Ellah shouts excitedly, pointing at the window.

We all run to the door.

"Sorry, I'm late," Nadav says, red-faced and panting. He stops to catch his breath as he steps through the door. "I just spoke with the golem. He's going to take me to the lake later."

We all clap our hands and take turns high-fiving Nadav.

We surround Miss Sara's desk and peer at the pages in the ancient book on golems.

"A worm in your mouth . . ." Ziv wrinkles up his nose. "I'm glad it's you and not me."

I punch Ziv in the arm and he winces.

"Okay, kids. We've got to come up with a plan," Miss Sara says.

I step forward. "First, we have this huge woven net that Ellah made." I hold it up for everyone to see.

Miss Sara leans closer to inspect the netting. "Nice workmanship."

"Thank you." Ellah glows.

"And we know how we're going to deal with the worm," I say. "Ellah offered us this little bag to catch the worm in and keep it in the water until the golem is on the ground. I think Ziv should be in charge of that once I get out of the water."

Ziv nods.

"Noam is here to use his clouds to darken the area around the lake so the golem won't suspect anything. And I think Noam can then help Ellah, who will be waiting up in a tree to throw the bag over the golem," I add.

"We need to get the golem to the lake," Miss Sara says.

"We're depending on Nadav to do that," I say.

Nadav steps forward. "I know that the golem likes Nurse Emunah. I've told him that we're going to meet her at the lake. He was pleased. I'm sure he'll take me there."

"Great." I breathe a sigh of relief.

"You've all read the golem book. To destroy the golem we have to de-create him. We have to do the opposite of what Lavan did to create him," Miss Sara points out.

Everyone nods.

"We'll do our best," I say.

"Come into the kitchen," Miss Sara says. "I have something to show you."

We all follow her into the kitchen. On the table in a blue dish are a bunch of chocolate chip cookies.

"Those look delicious," Ziv says as he reaches for one.

Miss Sara slaps his hand. "Those aren't for you. They're for the golem. All he has to do is eat one or two of them and he will find it hard to keep his eyes open."

We all gather around the table and stare at the innocent-looking cookies.

"The magic is in the dough. I ground up half a bottle of sleeping pills and mixed them inside the dough. These should make him really sleepy," Miss Sara explains. "Nadav, you take these along and offer them to the golem after you arrive at the lake."

Nadav nods.

"Just don't eat any. After you're finished, throw them into the lake. They should disintegrate quickly. The fish won't be affected by them."

Nadav salutes with the Israel Defense Forces salute – straight right hand with his middle finger touching his forehead.

"How did you get the golem to agree to take you to the lake?"

Nadav's face flushes. "He kind of owed me one," he says, and turns away from our curious eyes.

"Okay, kids. What time should we meet at the lake?" Miss Sara asks.

"The four of us should go there at two," Ellah says pointing at Noam, Ziv, and I. "Nadav, you should bring the golem at four after we've got everything set up."

Nadav nods.

"I'll meet you there before four just to make sure everything's in order," Miss Sara says.

We all agree.

"We'll see you there. Remember to bring the book," I say.

Miss Sara nods. "Of course."

We rehash our plan as we head out the door. I'm sure we kids can do this as long as I can get past the worm in my mouth. We really are going to mess up Lavan's plan. We might even become famous. My cheeks warm up as I imagine the news conference in which I explain how we destroyed the golem. But I don't mind the heat this time.

Chapter 34

Meeting at the Lake

"IT'S time for lunch," Ima calls up the stairs.

We slink down.

"I said lunch," Ima says, looking at us. "You guys are usually so hungry. What's the matter?"

Ziv and I exchange looks. "We're fine," I say. "We were busy upstairs."

Ima feels my forehead. "You're not getting sick, I hope."

"Don't worry," I reassure her, and kiss her on the cheek. "Miss Sara asked us to help her with something. We're going to be busy this afternoon."

"But remember tonight is the first night of Succot. You and Ziv should be home when the holiday starts."

"No problem, Mom."

We sit down at the kitchen table. Ima dishes up falafel, pitas, hummus, and Israeli salad – cucumber, tomato, and onion chopped up really small and mixed together. She sets a tall glass of cold milk in front of each of us.

We both stare at the food as though it's smelly liver and onions.

"Well, go ahead," Ima says.

We each pick up a pita and start filling it.

"Put the plates in the sink when you're finished," Ima calls to us. "I've got some work upstairs."

"I'm so nervous. It's hard to eat," I say after Ima goes back upstairs.

"Me too," Ziv agrees.

"Eat something so Ima doesn't worry." I pick up my pita and take a few bites. Ziv has a few bites, too, and then we put the rest of the food away in the fridge and take care of our dishes quickly.

"We're on our way," I call upstairs.

Ima comes out of her room. "Be careful and listen to Miss Sara, and get home on time."

"Don't worry, Ima. We'll be careful."

Ziv picks up his backpack and out we go. In the fresh air, both of us breathe a sigh of relief.

"You've got the stuff in your backpack?" I ask.

Ziv grins. "I've got the candles, matches, a flashlight, the worm bag. I brought a few granola bars and stuff. In case someone gets hungry."

"How can you think of granola bars at a time like this?" I shake my head.

We race to Noam and Ellah's house. We take the longer but less scary street route.

Our friends are waiting outside.

"Ready?" I ask.

"I guess so." Ellah's voice shakes a little. "I guess we're off to kill a golem. How freaky."

We all move toward the fields, too nervous to look at each other.

As we enter the forest, I remind everyone of the plan. "I'll go into the water and capture one of the worms. Noam, you climb the tree and start to darken the sky with your clouds . . . just like you did the night we went into the school."

"I wish you'd stop talking about that night," Ziv says.

"Sorry. Ellah, you're going to climb a tree opposite

Noam. How are you going to get the net bag to Noam from the tree?"

Ellah snorts. "I attached a long rope to the bag. He can climb holding his end of the rope and I'll hold the other end."

"Great." I heave a sigh of relief.

"Ziv, do you have the small bag for the worm?"

"It's in my backpack."

"Okay. You'll have to keep the worm in the water until we're ready to use it."

"No problem. I'm all set," Ziv says.

As we trek through the woods, all we can hear are the sounds of our shoes snapping twigs and our bodies rustling bushes.

"The last time we trekked through these woods we didn't even know what a golem was." Ellah's giggle doesn't sound like she's really amused.

We continue to tramp among the trees, pushing aside low-hanging branches and jumping through the tall grass.

"We've been walking for a while," Ellah says. "We should be getting close to the lake."

"It's just after those poisonous berry bushes up ahead. Remember we picked those berries last time we were here?" I ask.

Ellah nods.

"Anyone want a granola bar?" Ziv speaks up.

Noam rushes forward to get one from Ziv's backpack.

"Thanks," Noam says a moment later, his mouth full of crumbs.

After a short time, we can see the contour of the lake. The willows and sedge lining the surface have dwindled a little since the summer. We all look to the far side of the lake, where we first saw the man dressed in white.

"This is sooo weird," Ellah says softly. "I never wanted to see this place again. It was so scary last time."

"Don't worry. I'll take care of you," I blurt out. My cheeks heat up.

Ellah smiles her thanks and blushes, too.

I clear my throat. "Everyone get ready," I say. "Nadav and the golem should be here soon. I'm going to flow into the lake and capture one of those worms."

Chapter 35

A Captured Worm

I KICK off my sandals and sit down at the edge of the lake. I start to think of the words that make me dissolve into water. Flow, roll, blow, tumble . . . as the words run through my mind I begin to feel the slight tingling that happens before I become water. My arms and legs begin to loosen. I look into the lake, and then I'm the lake looking out over the bank. How do I get to the bottom of the lake without hands?

I float around the lake for a while. Then I have an idea.

I see Ziv step over to the edge of the lake. He's watching the water as it swirls around. I wonder if he can see which part is me. I swirl and swirl in great circles and begin flowing downward.

Through the bubbles and frothy water I see the muddy lake bottom. Green plants wave their stringy green leaves. Little silver fish dart back and forth. There are also deep red crawdads walking along on their jointed legs. I blow the water hard against the undersurface to stir the murky bottom. I see a couple of segmented worms hugging the bottom. These are the Oligochaeta ones Miss Sara described to me. What luck! I've uncovered two burrowing into the soil. These are the worms I'm looking for.

You're not going to get away from me, I think. I swish down, my water lips drawn back, my invisible mouth open. Slurp. Mud and plant leaves suck into my mouth. I close my mouth tightly. Something feels slimy between my teeth. I open my mouth. Half a worm floats up past my blinking eyes. I blow the water, mud, and leaves out of my mouth. The other half of the worm sails past. Ugh. I almost swallowed a worm. I can't do this.

I look up. I see my friends hanging over the side of the lake, looking down into the water. I sigh and push down again. I sweep toward the last remaining night crawler, my mouth open. I vacuum up the water and all the lake rubbish. The segmented body of the worm floats in through my lips. I carefully close my mouth and feel the worm moving up through the muddy silt and twisted leaves. Like an accordion, it stretches out and pulls itself together, moving on my tongue. A thick layer of silt settles on my tongue along with the creepy worm. I float over to the lake's edge. I slurp myself out of the water and lie like a puddle for a short moment. My parts re-form and I stand up.

Ziv rushes forward, and I carefully open my mouth.

Ziv holds back for a moment. "Ugghh," he says. He reaches into my mouth and feels around for the worm. I stand as still as I can. The slippery worm is under some leaves and dirt on the inside of my cheek. Ziv grabs it between his thumb and forefinger and pulls it out. He drops it into the mesh bag, ties a long string around it, and drops it back into the water.

I lurch over to the side of the lake, stomach heaving, and spit out green leaves and muddy silt. I'm going to throw up. Ellah runs up next to me with a water bottle. Thankfully, I gargle and rinse out my mouth, but I still have a silty feeling when I run my tongue along my gums.

"I'm glad that's over," are the only words I can get out.

Chapter 36

The Golem Arrives

I T'S five. Suddenly we hear the roar of a motorcycle approaching.

"That's them," I hiss. "Get to your places."

Noam is already on the limb of one of the trees, swirling clouds around in front of the moon. He holds the rope of the big mesh bag in his right hand. Ellah is sitting in the opposite tree holding on to the other side of the bag. I squat down behind a large shrub near the water's edge. Ziv sits next to me, holding on to the rope of the worm sack.

"Where's Miss Sara?" Ziv whispers.

I shrug. "I hope nothing's happened to her."

After a while we hear Nadav's voice. He's speaking to the golem. "Have a cookie," Nadav says. "They're really good."

There's a pause. We all hold our breath.

"You don't want a cookie? But they're delicious. See, I'm eating one."

I gasp.

"What's he doing?" I mouth.

Ziv shakes his head.

"Aren't they great?" Nadav asks the golem.

The golem answers with a snorty sound.

"Sure, help yourself to one," Nadav says. He's finally getting the golem to eat the poisoned cookies. "Have another one," he says.

I flash a wide grin at Ziv.

Nadav speaks again. "You're right. I haven't finished mine yet. Oops, it dropped. It's okay. No problem, I've got more."

I beam. Nadav has this under control.

Nadav keeps talking and I can hear Chaim's grunting replies. The voices get louder. They're getting closer.

Hands shaking, hardly breathing, I wait for the golem to walk under the trees and get caught in the net. In the dim light we see his huge hulking form clomp to the lake's edge. Oh my gosh, Nadav didn't take him through the trees! We're not going to be able to use the net. Now what?

My heart beats wildly while we all wait. What's Nadav going to do? I stare at Nadav's back.

"Look!" Nadav is pointing to the middle of the lake. "Is that an octopus?"

An octopus in the lake. Is he crazy?

The golem leans far over the edge of the lake, looking for the phantom octopus. Nadav hurries up behind him, and with a tremendous shove, he pushes the golem into the water. The golem sinks below the surface quickly. Maybe he's too shocked to try and swim.

I jump up. I've got to get into the water. My water words roll through my head. I slide across the grassy bank and into the lake. I see the golem. He is kicking his feet and waving his hands. He's rising to the surface. Plants and dirt whirl around his body. I swirl the water over him, forcing him below the surface again.

I hear Ellah from far above. "Push him out with a wave," she yells.

I bounce around under the golem. As Nadav counts to three, I buoy the golem up with a big swell of water and he rolls out of the lake. I gather myself together and spill out after him. Ellah is staring at me as I re-form.

"He's coughing up lake water! He needs help," Ellah says as she rushes over. I roll my eyes and draw my finger across my throat to remind Ellah why we're here.

Suddenly the golem stands up. He shakes the water out of his hair like a dog, then turns and faces us. He raises his fists like a boxer and charges. I zigzag away, but he catches Ellah by the hair. She starts screaming as he drags her toward the water.

My heart is pounding. I have to save Ellah. I charge forward and punch the golem in the stomach. My fist feels like I've hit a steel drum. He drops Ellah's hair and turns toward me, staring, eyes dilated like an enraged bulldog. Ellah struggles to her feet and races into the woods.

The golem rushes toward me.

"Under the trees!" Nadav yells.

I spin on my heels and charge under the trees. The golem is so close his hot breath burns my neck. I lunge forward. Two steps ahead of him, I dodge to the left.

"Now! Drop the net." Nadav's voice rings out.

Whoosh! The net drops out of the tree like a butterfly trap.

I hear a cry behind me and I spin around. The golem is standing, thrashing under the trees, wrapped in the net.

"We've got him," Noam yells.

"Not till he's down and out," I shout. "Be careful."

As I step closer, the golem's legs buckle and he falls to his knees. A foolish look crosses his face. He seems drunk. The cookies are finally working.

Noam slides down the tree. Ellah inches out of the woods. We're all staring at the golem.

Ziv calls from the lake. "Are you ready for the worm?"

"Lay him down first," I yell. "I see the cookies are taking effect."

As I watch the golem, he falls backwards onto the ground.

"Pull him out from under the trees. Get him closer to the water." Everyone follows my instructions and drags him forward, each one grabbing a limb.

"He weighs a ton," Ellah gasps.

The golem twitches and exhales deeply. He tries to roll over. I jerk backwards. He's waking up.

"Help!" the golem yells. He pushes at the tangle of net and tries to stand.

We all grab a corner of the net. We kneel and hold it low to the ground to keep him down, but he's too strong for us. He stands up, throwing us all backwards. He whips his arms around.

"Watch out!" I yell. "He's getting loose."

Through the net, the golem grabs Ziv by the neck. I rush forward. I pound on the golem's back, but my hits just bounce off him.

Ziv's raw breaths rattle my ears.

"Use your gift!" Ellah yells.

Water words fill my mind. I'm a tsunami. The golem is knocked back off his feet, and for a split second I admire my best wave yet. Then the golem loses his grip on Ziv. I wash Ziv away from him and cradle him so he can land gently. Then I re-form as quickly as I can.

I run forward and rip open my backpack. "I tug out the small paper packet and the spray bottle Miss Sara handed to me as I left her house. Then I kneel down by the lakeside and gather a small amount of water to mix with the powder. I screw on the spray top.

Shaking the bottle, I yell, "I'll squirt him with this."

The golem is fighting us inside the net. As he rises up, Nadav, Noam, and Ellah tighten their hold on the net.

I crank the bottle several times and spray a mist over the golem. A smell of green herbs rises from his body.

The effect is instantaneous. The golem falls backwards. He's asleep.

"You kids are amazing." Miss Sara's voice fills the glen. "Sorry I'm late, but you've done a great job." She rushes forward, the big green book in her arms. She places the book carefully on the ground and opens it. She flips to the back of the book and searches for something on one of the pages. "Here it is," she says as she points to a particular paragraph. Miss Sara rummages through her backpack. She hands me a candle and some matches. She hands a frame drum to Nadav and gives a *shofar* to Ziv. To Noam she hands a triangle and a wooden stick, and to Ellah a recorder.

"You must walk around the golem counterclockwise, the opposite direction Lavan used to create it," Miss Sara says.

We begin to circle counterclockwise around the helpless sleeping golem. Around and around we go. We circle its body seven times.

Nadav beats a slow rhythm on the drum. Ziv blows short blasts on the *shofar*, which we last heard at the end of *Yom Kippur,* a few days ago. Noam dings the triangle and Ellah plays a mournful tune on the recorder. I stand close to Miss Sara and light my candle. She begins to recite:

"Lord of Understanding, here lies the golem, powerless and alone. Consider him masterless. Remove him from this world. Annul him like the dust of the earth."

As she repeats the words, heavy clouds rush in and cover the sun. A blast of air blows out my candle. Darkness descends.

"He's beginning to move," Nadav, the only one who can see clearly in the dark, whispers to us.

"We must work quickly," Miss Sara says. "Relight the candle," she orders. I follow her instructions. She says, "Ziv, bring the bag with the worm as fast as you can."

Ziv fishes the worm bag out of the water and runs forward, holding it carefully. I hand the candle to Noam and reach inside the bag. I shudder as the worm contracts, expands, and crawls over my hand. I grab it and lay it on the letter R. The worm slips off the letter and starts wiggling down the golem's face. A shiny trail of yellow goo slides down the left side of the golem's cheek. I pick up the worm's wiggly body and place it back on the R. Suddenly the worm collapses. More yellowish puss leaks from its body.

As we watch, the R begins to shrivel up and disappear. Slowly, the golem begins to disintegrate.

Wide-eyed, we stand frozen. We can't tear our eyes away. In the flicker of candlelight, we watch as the golem's fingers and toes become clumps of dirt. His pant legs flatten out. His hips and chest collapse. And then his eyes, nose, and mouth are wiped off his face. In only five minutes, the body of the golem has gone back to the dirt it was. In the breeze, his empty clothes blow away into the lake. All that's left of the golem are a few small mounds of dirt.

We all collapse to the ground, exhausted. Completely silent, I blink, still thinking about the scene we just witnessed.

Ellah begins to cry. The sound rouses us from our stupor. I look up and crawl over to take Ellah's hand. "Don't cry. It's okay," I say again and again. "It wasn't a real person," I try to explain. "It was like a ghost walking among us."

"Do you know why I was late getting the golem to the lake?" Nadav asks.

Everyone turns to listen.

"We were late because the golem had been given other plans for tonight. Guess what he was going to do?"

We shrug.

"He was going to kidnap Eden. His plan was to give her to Lavan."

"That loser," Noam mutters.

"Really?" Ellah asks.

Nadav nods.

"You children have saved Kfar Keshet from a terrible disaster," Miss Sara says. "Lavan will be weakened by the destruction of this golem, but he still has power and he still has plans to wreck us. We all have to be on guard."

I'm too freaked out to whoop or holler. My brain is whizzing around in overdrive. Images of the golem disappearing into the dirt jump before my eyes. I look at my friends. They have dazed looks on their faces, too.

"Gather some wood, dears." Miss Sara's voice breaks the silence. "We need to build a bonfire. There's one more thing we have to do now before we go home."

We all move toward the trees. In a few minutes I've found a load of kindling and a small log. I place some rocks in a circle and put the kindling inside. Ellah drops some more kindling and a few pinecones on top of mine. Ziv and Noam drag forward a really large log. I start the fire.

Where's Nadav? I look around but I don't see him. He must still be collecting wood.

We sit down around the fire. Miss Sara takes out the green book again and turns to the very last pages. She looks up and smiles. "There is a particular ceremony to be performed on the death of a golem," she says as she points to the page in the book.

We all lean forward.

"Jordan, you caught the worm and put it on the golem's forehead."

I nod. My stomach flips a little as I remember the sensation of the worm crawling around in my mouth.

"Take some of this powder and throw it onto the fire."

I take a pinch of orange powder from the plastic bag that has been passed to me and I toss it on the flames. A long, twisting, neon-green-colored worm appears in the fire. It looks like the worm I brought up from the lake. How did Miss Sara do that?

"Ellah, you wove the net that caught the golem."

Ellah nods.

"Throw a pinch of the powder into the flames."

Ellah throws her pinch in, and instantly, purple strands of fire weave themselves into a net and then disappear.

"Ziv, you guarded the worm in the water."

Ziv's pinch of powder creates a blue puddle of water that looks like the lake. And then Noam's pinch of powder makes a billowing white cloud.

The fire and the glowing symbols have calmed us down.

"What's Nadav supposed to do with the powder?" Ellah asks.

I pull in my lower lip. He brought the golem to us. He should have a part in the ceremony.

"Where is Nadav, anyways?" Noam asks.

We all look around.

"My color sense says he's up there," Ziv whispers to me. He points to one of the pine trees.

I stand up and walk toward the tree. I can see where he's sitting. Really high up, almost at the top. I'm glad I spent so much time in trees when I was trying to fly. I grab hold of the trunk and hoist myself up. Higher and higher I pull myself through the branches. When I'm at the same level he is, I sit down on a branch.

"What's happening?" I ask.

"Nothing."

I hear hurt in his voice. "Why aren't you down doing the ceremony with us?"

"I kind of feel like I don't belong . . . all you . . . brothers and sisters down there. And I didn't actually do anything so much."

"Are you kidding?" The surprise I'm feeling is sincere; it almost knocks me out of the tree. "You brought the golem to us! That was huge."

"So I'm going to drop some of that powder in to the fire and it's going to make a foot? Give me a break."

"Come on, Nadav, what you did was really important."

Nadav shrugs his shoulders. I can tell that he's not buying it.

"I'll race you down," I say, hoping he'll join me.

"Okay," he says at last. "You go first."

I start to slip out of the tree. I'm assuming Nadav is behind me. After a minute or two, I look up, but I don't see him anywhere. Then there is a sudden roar. It's the sound of a motorcycle. Nadav has left the party.

I return to the fire, alone. I'm feeling sad. I sort of like Nadav even though he's a bit snooty.

Miss Sara nods to me and I know she's guessed what happened with Nadav. She stands up, holding the bag with the remainder of the powder. With a big swing she scatters the powder. There is a big flash. Kfar Keshet appears right before our eyes, topped by a huge rainbow. The image lasts for several moments and then disappears into the fire.

"You've saved our village from a great disaster. The golem was a dangerous and powerful tool in Lavan's hands. Without him, Lavan will have to move more carefully, and so will we," Miss Sara says. "God bless you."

I'm so proud. My chest fills out all the empty space in my tee shirt. My best friends and I have saved Kfar Keshet. We used our special gifts and worked together. I look around. Everyone is smiling.

I throw my hands up into the air. "Hurrah," I yell.

"Hurrah," my friends yell back.

We gather in a circle, slap hands, and dance around the glowing fire. As the fire burns down, we throw as much water on it as we can. Then we all head back to Kfar Keshet so that we can go back to our homes, sit in our *succot*, and celebrate the beginning of our holiday.

In Lavan's Study

I N Lavan's study a desk lamp illuminates the room. Scattered papers cover the rug. A cup of coffee has overturned on some books that lie jumbled on the floor. The phone receiver dangles over the edge of the desk, emitting a low siren sound, waiting to be hung up.

A body lies across the desk. It's Lavan. He is gasping for breath. Spit rolls out of the corner of his mouth and oozes onto his desk blotter. He is groaning and rubbing his hand over his burning forehead. *Aagarrah, I'm dying.* He rolls to the side, knocking his desk lamp to the floor. Random thoughts run through his muddled brain. *DREAD, DEAD . . . words, words? I have to pull myself up.*

He braces his hands on his desk and tries to lift his body. After a fraction of a second he falls back again, too weak to rise. He lies there for a few minutes, trying to figure out what is happening.

He rolls his head from side to side. Then he freezes. His eyes widen. He focuses on his coat rack, on his white caftan hanging there. His hand again wanders over the burning skin on his forehead. The fog in his brain is clearing.

I wore my caftan. Why? He rubs his forehead again and then he remembers. *Something's happened to my golem . . .*

to my creation. Impossible! He tries to rise, but once again falls backwards. Lying there, he knows his golem has been destroyed. He is suffering like the golem has suffered.

How did they do it? He wonders. Tears fill his eyes. *I'll never be able to create another one . . . too much time, too much energy.*

He chases the memories that wheel around his brain.

There's a nosy Kfar Keshet kid, he remembers. The golem thought the kid knew about the word on his forehead. Lavan scratches his head. What was his name? That kid with the weird black eyes. Sitting with his back propped up against a wall, he thinks, slowly and carefully. His name started with an N. He sits quietly for a long time. In a flash he remembers the name. It's Nadav.

Wait till I get my hands on you, he thinks. *You'll pay for what you've done.*

Acknowledgements

WRITING a novel is a collective endeavor and I have been blessed with the help and support of a myriad of people.

From the very beginning, Arnold and Tamar Goldman-Sachs have listened to every word and have offered both helpful suggestions and unswerving support.

An armful of kisses to my niece, Deborah Goldman, who has taken my dream and successfully made it a reality.

Kudos to Deborah's army of supporters: Lori Carlson, my creative book designer; Molly Woodward, Heather Young, and Dana Baker-Williams, my perfectionist editors.

My endless appreciation to Rachel Moseley, my talented illustrator, who made the story of Kfar Keshet come to life.

To Beth Barany, my gratitude for working and reworking my drafts, always aiming for perfection.

A big round of applause to Deborah Meghnagi Bailey who worked on the 'final' manuscript to make it, finally, the 'final' for her insightful questions and persistent search for the best.

A big thank you to Marissa Newman for always saying "yes, we can do that," at each stage of the publishing process.

My appreciation to David Brauner and his outstanding writers group who supported and challenged every chapter.

And a big thank you to my friend Caren Neuman who read and reread every version of this book.

To Guy Shulman, who early on, suggested the need for more tension in the story and thus, like Lavan, created the golem.

To Summer Laurie who critiqued my manuscript at the BookPassages Children's Bookwriter's Conference and left me with a need to change a major part of my plot.

To Yocheved Zemel who listened to and added her helpful suggestions to my final manuscript.

And to Elad, Hod, Rephael, Sophie, Leviel, Tuvia, and Natanel who are waiting to have starring roles in my next books.